BAIT

A BADGERS CROSSING NOVELLA

and bonus story:

ELEANOR CULPEPPER
& THE CROSSROADS BOOK

Paperback: ISBN 978-1-7393756-0-7
First paperback edition May 2023

Edited by Imogen Peniston (Greenteeth Press),
Peter Laws and Kirsty Childs.
Layout, design, illustrations and cover art by Paul Childs
except *Beware The Conductor'* (page 127)
by Christopher Fieldhouse.

Published by Broccton Press.

PaulChilds.co.uk
BrocctonPress.co.uk
BadgersCrossing.co.uk

This is for anyone who:

Played out in the woods on their bikes all day
and still got home in time for The A-Team;

Survived the many deadly hazards of daily life thanks to the
lifesaving advice of Public Information Films;

Watched *Children of the Stones*, *Dramarama*, *Look & Read* and
The Children's Film Foundation (not to mention its harder cousin,
The Children's Film Unit) through their fingers;

Hid beneath their sheets after bedtime, secretly reading comics like
Misty, *2000AD*, *Jinty* or *Scream!* by torchlight.

And if you like badgers.
There are quite a few badgers in this book.

And:

Bob Fischer.
Thanks for helping the kids of *The Haunted Generation*
find each other again - HauntedGeneration.co.uk

***

The students from Lodge Park Academy.
If I can do this, you can too: #CorbyKidsCan

***

My lovely wife Kirsty.
You keep me going. Love you loads.

CONTENTS

BAIT

PART I:
GHOSTS

SEARCHING

Now: Thursday, 22nd April 2021

"Are ghosts real, Dad?"

There were many questions Tim expected, hoped and even prepared for Debbie to ask, but that was not one of them. Although he tried to react to it in as normal a manner as he could, he still found himself shifting in his seat.

How do I answer this without lying or scaring her? he thought.

He looked at her but didn't really see her. His mind was elsewhere, back in the school holidays of 1988 and that day in Weaver Woods; the clearing with its crumbling shack, the decomposing door creaking open and Claire's hand beckoning him from its shadowy threshold. He pictured himself reaching out to her, getting so close he could almost feel her and then— the chill in his stomach, back and legs when he'd seen the real Claire standing on the edge of the clearing by the treeline, smiling and waving to him.

Tim shivered. He hadn't thought about it in a couple of years but those three simple words brought it all back as if it were yesterday.

Are ghosts real?

Fighting off more than thirty years of memories, of waking drenched in sweat, paralysed with fear, thinking that the hand, that dreadful gnarled, clawed hand was reaching for him, he patted the cushion beside him. Debbie leapt up onto the sofa and snuggled into him.

One day I'll tell her about what I saw, or thought I saw, he thought. *The cabin, the ghost of Patience Starling. But not today.*

"Why do you ask Deb?" He rubbed her shoulder. "Is it because of what happened to Bert?"

Debbie shook her head.

He took her hand. "It's natural to ask questions like that when someone dies. It's only been a few weeks so—"

"No. It's not Bert," she said, pulling her hand away to scratch her cheek, just like her mother always used to. "Bert wasn't into ghosts and heaven and hell and all that stuff."

"So what did he believe?"

"He said that after he died he'd go back into the land and become a part of it."

"Ah, okay, I think I understand." He smiled at her, desperate to lighten the mood. He really didn't want to be talking about this but he knew he had to. It was important to his daughter. "Like Mufasa in The Lion King?"

"Yes!" she said. "Exactly like The Lion King!" She laughed. "Except with less lions and more badgers and squirrels and stuff." She leaned into him and took his hand again. "I'm talking about The Conductor."

"The Conductor?" Tim said. He pulled his hand away. The hairs on his arms stood on end and he felt a tingle of icy cold run through his entire body. "Where did you hear—"

"At school," she said. "He's supposed to be the ghost

of some old railway worker–"

"I know who he is," he said. He paused and chuckled. "That old story was going around when I was your age. We used to say that he took away naughty kids who played on the railway tracks."

"That's what someone at school told me too," she said.

He pulled her into his side and she laid her head on his shoulder.

"I'm going to tell you something a little bit gruesome now. Are you ready for it?"

She nodded. He felt her shiver.

"Okay, here we go. A boy who went to my school - about four or five years before I started going there - was messing about on the tracks with his little sister and they got hit by a train. I'm pretty sure it was part of the reason they closed the railway down. I never met him, but even years later the story going around the playground was that The Conductor took their souls as punishment."

He felt Debbie grip his arm tightly. He turned to her. She looked back into his eyes, her face full of concern and worry.

"Do you think he's real, Dad?"

"Listen to me, Debbie," he rubbed her arm. "That's what they call an urban legend, which means that the only place The Conductor exists is in stories, and the only reason he still exists is that people keep telling those stories. He started off as a character on TV. Did you know that?"

She shook her head.

"Yeah, it was an advert they used to show on kids' TV, to stop children playing on railways. I think the schoolyard stories might have been started by parents who'd seen it, to scare their children into behaving. 'Don't go onto the train line or The Conductor will get you,' they used to say. Your granny certainly said it to me a few times, although I never saw him. Not once." He winked at her. "Even when I did play on the tracks!"

She giggled and elbowed him in the ribs. "You're so bad, Dad!" She released his hand, pushed herself up from the sofa and turned to face him. "So what you're telling me is that there's no such thing as The Conductor?"

"Exactly!" He leaned back, relieved that he hadn't needed to lie after all. "There is definitely no such thing as The Conductor."

"Oh, that's good," she said. "Because the other day Sophia's big sisters took us down to the old tunnel and—"

"Hang on—"

"Yeah. And we were playing Spin The Bottle by the old boarded-up tunnel and I thought I could hear someone in there whistling and Nicola told us it was The Conductor and Rachel said he was coming to get Sophia and me for being brats so we ran away. But if he's not real, then that's okay, yeah?"

Before Tim could speak she rushed out of the room and stomped up the stairs.

"Wait." He leapt out of his seat and rushed after her but the bedroom door had already slammed shut. He yelled up the stairs, "You were doing WHAT?"

CHANGING PLANS

Four Weeks Ago

The hospital made Debbie think of that time one of the kids in her class had thrown up on the school hall floor during P.E. Their teacher, Mrs McGann, made them all sit on the mats while she fetched a mop and bucket. The cleaning fluid, mixed with the contents of Oscar Palmer's stomach, created sharp, eye-watering fumes that scorched the back of her throat.

This hospital ward had that same stench. Like someone had tried to conceal sickness but had failed spectacularly. This time, however, it wasn't because someone had devoured too many Foamy Shrimps at break time.

From a chair by the nurse's station, she watched her dad. He was sitting beside Bert, talking, nodding, occasionally laughing with little humour, and sometimes it looked like they were disagreeing. Her dad was shaking his head. What were they saying? And more importantly, why had Bert asked to see her dad alone for a moment. Why not her?

It wasn't fair.

She stared at them. The stare slowly transformed into a glare. The glare started to blur as tears began to form in the corners of her eyes, stinging them.

They were both keeping something from her, but what was it? She hated not knowing.

After what felt like hours, her dad stood up, patted Bert's hand and headed back to the ward entrance. She leapt from her chair and placed a hand on her hip, ready to lay into him for keeping her waiting so long.

He immediately slumped into the empty seat and rested his head in his hands.

"He wants to talk to you, Debbie," he said. "Alone. I'll wait here and–"

She spun around and ran into the ward, her trainers squeaking fast on the shiny linoleum floor.

Bert's eyes lit up as she entered the ward.

"Ah, young Debbie! Come on in! Sit with me a while, brighten my day," That smile, still so full of joy, normally made her return a huge grin but now her mouth was a thin line and her forehead was banded with deep wrinkles as she tried hard to hold back tears. She sat at his side and put her hand on his, careful not to knock the cannula jutting out.

"Hey, What's all this? What's the matter littl'un?"

"Are you going to..." she sniffed, "die?"

That last word, the one she'd been so afraid of even thinking, was finally said and she couldn't hold the tears back any longer. She leaned into him and sobbed into his shoulder.

"There now. What's this?" Bert stroked her hair. "Don't you cry. I've had a good, long life and my time's almost up - but meeting you and your dad has made the last few years some of the best!"

"But... but..." the sobs increased in volume until they had turned into a shout. "It's not FAIR!"

The other patients in the ward glanced up from their

grapes and Sudoku books.

She lowered her voice to little more than a whisper.

"I feel like I've only just met you and now I'm losing you. I want more time. I need more time."

"I know, I know," Bert continued to stroke her hair and handed her a tissue from a box on his bedside cabinet. She wiped the tears from her cheeks, blew her nose and handed the soiled paper back to Bert, who picked it up by the corner and dropped it into a waste bin at the side of his bed.

"I've not got a lot of time left," he said. "But I've known this was coming for a while and I've had time to make some, er, preparations, shall we say?"

She sniffed again and tilted her head. "Preparations for what?"

"Your dad won't tell you this yet, and I promised him I wouldn't tell you, but guess what?"

"What?"

He held up his left hand. The index and middle fingers were crossed. Debbie instantly recognised this symbol and knew she was about to be told something she shouldn't know. Something cool.

"But you must promise me something," he said.

She nodded. "Okay."

"Good. Then listen carefully. This is top secret."

She looked over her shoulder. Tim was sitting in the corridor flicking through a car magazine. She pulled her chair closer to Bert's bedside and leaned in close to his face.

"After I'm gone you're going to get a letter from a solicitor. Do you know what one of those is?"

She nodded.

"In that letter will be the details of my will. Now, listen. I lived on my own for many years, and I've had no other family to speak of in a long while. And that means—"

"What does it mean, Bert?"

He chuckled and patted her hand.

"It means that I'm going to leave everything I own," he paused and winked. "To you."

Her gasp was so loud that the nosy patients looked her way again.

"Everything?"

"Well, there are a few things you wouldn't be interested in. A lovely young lady is taking Fran, my motorcycle, and I know she'll be well looked after. There's still my Land Rover and a few other bits but I'll have them sold off. They'll be no good to you now anyway. Best someone else gets the benefit from them while they're still running."

"But what about the house? I'm only ten! I'm far too young to own a house!"

"What money I have left over after legal fees will be divided up. Some of it will be shared amongst my closest friends. Some will be used on the upkeep of the house and the rest will be put in a trust fund for you. It's like a savings account that you'll be allowed to access when you're eighteen, along with the deeds to the house."

"So if my dad knows all this then there must be some other secret, right?"

He winked. "You always were a sharp one, young Deborah."

She smiled. Bert was, after all, the only person she ever let get away with calling her by her full name. Not even her dad. Especially her dad!

"Yes, your father will have to sign a few forms and act as trustee until you're old enough. He said it was too much, that it would spoil you, but deep down I know he was grateful. That's not the big secret."

"Then what is?"

"This."

He reached into his bedside cabinet and pulled out something Debbie was very familiar with; a walking stick with a badger's head carved into the handle.

"Your cane? What's so secret about that?"

"Shhh." He grinned at her. "Watch closely."

He put his two thumbs into the badger's mouth and pulled the jaws apart. The head swung wide open on a hidden hinge that Debbie had never noticed, despite having used the cane on countless woodland hikes. He then grasped the shaft of the cane with both hands and twisted.

A small silver key slowly rose out of the centre of the cane. To Debbie, it seemed like a fairly unremarkable, modern-looking key for such a cool, mysterious hiding place.

"Is that–"

"Yup!" Bert was smiling as he pulled the key out of its housing and held it up for a few seconds so the ward's fluorescent lights reflected off it, giving it a magical glow.

"This is the spare key to my front door." He slotted the key back into the middle of the cane, pressed it down with his thumb and snapped the badger's head shut with a click.

"I used to have another," he said as he handed her the cane. She took it, eyes wide with awe and reverence. "Lost it hiking along the railway in the woods when I was just a young man. I was devastated, of course. They were handmade, only two of them in the whole world. One for me and one for my Pa. He gave me his own one when he saw how upset I was, and I've been very careful never to let this one out of my sight ever since. Do you think you can look after this, as a way to honour me?"

She nodded.

"Good, good! I knew I could trust you. And that's why I want you to do something very important for me."

"Anything."

"I'd like for you to carry on with everything I taught you. Caring for the badgers, the trees, the harvest, everything."

"But I can't do it without you."

"Oh Deborah," he took her hand. "I've been watching you as we've been out in the forest. You *have* been doing it. You've not needed my help for months now."

"Well, I suppose, but–"

"No buts! It's true! You'll need to use my house, and you can do so whenever you wish. It will be cleaned a few times a year. The electricity, water and internet will be kept on and you already have the Wi-Fi password. If you're struggling or you get a little frightened, I've written some instructions just for you on my computer. You'll know where to find them when you start it up."

A tear slid down her face and dropped off of her cheek

onto Bert's hand.

"I know it's a big ask, especially keeping something like this from your dad, but I know I can trust you. He doesn't quite understand the land in the way you do and the forest needs tending now. It won't wait until you're eighteen."

"I'll do it!" Her reply almost slipped out as a shout again. She quickly looked over her shoulder at her dad who looked up from his magazine and gave her a sympathetic wave. She raised a hand and he delved back into the magazine.

"I'll do it," she whispered. She turned back to Bert who handed her the cane.

"Take this, it'll be listed in the will, but you should have it now."

"No. No. You'll need it when you get out of–"

"I think we both know I won't be leaving this place. Not on my feet at least."

Tears, a lot more of them, began to pool in her eyes again.

"Oh, come now," Bert said as she collapsed into him. She threw her arms around him and wept into his chest, knowing in her heart that this would be the last time she'd see him. He patted her on the back as tears formed in his own eyes.

After a few minutes of holding each other in silence, Tim came into the ward. He crouched down beside her and gently rested his hand on her back. She lifted her head and looked into his eyes.

"Come on, now Deb. Visiting time's over. These people need to get some sleep."

"Bert!" She clung to him. "I don't want to go. Don't make me!"

He patted her hand.

"It's okay. You go now, and remember everything I told you, yes?"

She sniffed back the tears and nodded. Finally, she slid the chair back from the bed with a screech and stood up, holding the cane tight to her chest.

"Bert, I guess this is goodbye." Tim held out his hand.

He took it but the cannula in the back of his own hand prevented him from gripping it too tightly. "Aye. Goodbye Tim Carter. You're a good man, and you've raised a fine young lady you can be proud of."

Tim nodded. "Thank you."

Bert took a breath before turning to Debbie.

"Goodbye, Deborah Carter." His voice was a whisper. "It has been a genuine pleasure to know you. I wasn't blessed with grandchildren of my own, not until that day I found you lost in the woods, and I couldn't have wished for anyone better."

She pressed her lips together tight and was unable to say anything for a moment. Instead, she leant down and kissed the back of his hand. She brought herself under control for long enough to speak one more time.

"I never met either of my grandpas, so I'm glad you found us. Goodbye Bert."

He winked at her.

She was too sad to smile back properly, but she tried anyway and his face lit up one last time like it always did when she answered the door to her. Tim placed a hand on her shoulder and firmly but gently guided her away from the bed and out of the ward. As they were leaving she glanced back over her shoulder one last time to wave goodbye, but Bert was already sleeping.

HOW TO USE THE TELEPHONE

Now: Friday, 23rd April 2021

"Dad? I'm going to stay at Ty's house tonight, okay?" Debbie called as she slammed the door behind her.

The door swung open before she'd even made it to her BMX bike in the garden.

"Woah, woah, woah, young lady!" Tim looked down the steps at her and sighed. She was prepared for an overnight stay. Her backpack was full to bursting with goodness knows what and she had her hiking boots and socks on.

"What?" She thrust her badger-head cane into the ground, leaned on it and glared at him. He tried not to laugh. She looked like Robin Hood standing up to the Sheriff in one of the old movies that they'd watched together.

He paused.

"How about asking me *before* you're already on your way there?" he said.

"Dad?" She put on her favourite sweet-but-sarcastic voice. "Can I stay at Ty's tonight?"

He made a show of rubbing his chin slowly and raised his eyes skyward. His classic way of letting her know that he'd think about it. Finally, he looked back at her and said "Well–"

"Oh, go on Dad! It's not fair!"

"I haven't said anything yet," he laughed. "What does Ty's mum say?"

"She says it's fine." She answered quickly. *Too quickly*, he thought.

"Well let's see, shall we? Back in the house young lady." He held the door open as she stormed up the steps. She stomped down the hallway, turned around and glared at her dad. Tim pulled his phone from his pocket and sat on the bottom step, glaring back at her as he dialled the number.

It went straight to voicemail so he hung up and tried the landline instead.

When it began to ring he pressed the speakerphone button. Debbie was drumming her fingers on the bannister. Impatience? Or nervousness? He wasn't sure.

After a few rings, there was a click. The voice at the other end said: "Hello? Grant household."

"Oh, hi 'Manda. It's me."

"Mr Carter?"

"Mr Carter?" he laughed. "I thought we were a little bit beyond the formal stage by now!"

"Oh, uh, sorry, Tim. Busy day at school. Still got my teacher head on. You know what it's like."

"I thought you were working late tonight. I was just going to leave a message asking you to call me back when you got home but since you've decided to knock off early... Or did they give you time off for good behaviour, Hedgehog?"

He winked at Debbie, who from the look on her face was disgusted. He could imagine what she was thinking and he stifled a laugh.

She put a finger down her throat and shook her head at him. Then she whispered into his ear so Amanda wouldn't hear. "Keep your cute nicknames to yourself, please,"

He held up a finger to his mouth and whispered back. "Shhh. I'm trying to listen."

"What was that?"

"Nothing. Sorry. I think I ought to tell you that you're on speakerphone and my angelic daughter–"

"Hi!" Debbie chipped in cheerily.

"...is listening in too. She seems to think that you've said it's okay for her to stay over tonight. I caught her about to head on over there on her bike with enough luggage for a fortnight."

A pause and was that... a giggle? A cough?

"Are you alright, 'Manda?"

"Er. yeah. Fine. Just not feeling great. That's why I'm home from work early. It's no problem. As long as they keep the noise down and go to bed at a reasonable hour, I'm good with it."

"You sure? Last thing you want if you're not up to it is Little Miss Loudspeaker here keeping you–"

Debbie poked her tongue out at him

"Keeping you awake all night."

"Honestly Tim, it's no problem. I've got enough food in the freezer to feed an army, so they can help themselves."

"Okay then," He paused. "Are you sure everything is alright? You don't sound yourself."

"I'm fine, honestly. I've just had a busy week. I'll be okay."

"Alright then." He paused. "Let's go out again next week when you're feeling better, yeah? I quite fancy that new Portuguese place in town."

"Sounds great. We'll talk about it later, okay?"

"Er. Yeah. Okay. Talk soon. Love—"

Click.

He stared at the handset for several seconds, perplexed at what had just happened. Amanda really didn't sound right at all.

"Perhaps I should take you over there myself, make sure she's alright," he said to Debbie.

"I'm going on my bike, Dad! It'll be fine. I'll be fine. She'll be fine. Everything. Will. Be. Fine." She tapped the rhythm of each word out on the banister.

"I'll let you know if there's any problems, okay? You just have a nice relaxing night off from, what did you call me? Little Miss Loudspeaker? Rude, much?"

He studied her for a moment. She wasn't a little girl anymore. Physically, yes, she still was, but the way she held herself and the way she spoke to him was so grown up now, and he wasn't ready for that yet. He knew she'd be perfectly capable of cycling the mile or so to Ty's house. Taking her there himself wasn't so much for her benefit as his, to prove to himself that she still needed him.

And it broke him a little that she didn't.

MAGPIES

Two Weeks Ago

One of Ernie Hunt's greatest pleasures was sitting out on his garden patio on a Sunday morning and reading the newspapers over breakfast. Although he could afford to have pretty much anything he wanted delivered straight to his mansion, his absolute favourite was a good old fashioned fry up from Gary's Café in the village.

Today was a special day. The sun was shining, the birds were singing, Frankie the pug was trotting obediently at his side and Tania was up from London for a few weeks. He took a deep breath of that lovely countryside air and let out a huge sigh of contentment as he carried the three takeaway meals home. He entered the security code on the gate and whistled a tune as they slowly swung open - Barry Manilow's *Can't Smile Without You*, an unofficial anthem of his beloved Tottenham Hotspur.

Ernie balanced the food boxes on his elbow as he unlocked the door with a key that had been hanging around his neck on a lanyard. He unhooked the lead from Frankie's collar. The dog trotted into the hallway and Ernie followed, slamming the door shut with the heel of his boot. He entered the kitchen as his wife, Liz, poured coffee into three cups. Ernie smiled when he noticed that one of them was his commemorative 1966/67 FA Cup Final mug.

"Somebody's in a good mood," she said.

"You bet I am!" He winked at her. Elizabeth Wilde was every bit as stunning as the day he'd met her.

And what a day. He glanced at a framed photograph on the wall. Spurs captain Dave Mackay, raised on the shoulders of his teammates, triumphantly holding the FA Cup aloft. Ernie looked beyond the players and the officials, at the mass of faces making up the crowd. No matter how hard he looked, he could never spot himself and Liz enjoying their first-ever date, but he knew they were there, hidden somewhere in the crowd.

Ernie didn't realise he'd been staring at the photo for so long until Liz waved a hand over his face.

"Are you alright Ern?" she said, rubbing his shoulder. "Can I get you anything?"

"No, love," he said. "I've got everything I need right here. A lovely home, my beautiful girls, Frankie and..." he produced the cardboard boxes from behind his back and held them up with a grin. "Three of Gary's finest Full English breakfasts." He sniffed the air above the boxes and let out a long, luxurious "Aaaah."

"Take those to the patio. Tan's still in bed - didn't get here until after midnight, poor thing. I'll get her up and bring these through in a minute." She nodded to the steaming coffee cups.

Ernie winked at her and opened the patio door.

"Come on Frankie. There's a good boy."

The dog grunted and wheezed as it followed him into the garden, hoping to score a rasher of bacon.

"Tania," he heard Liz holler into the hallway. "Breakfast!"

"I'll be down in a minute, Mum," came a voice from upstairs.

"Okay! Can you grab the newspapers on your way?"

"Will do!"

Ernie's knees creaked like an old rope as he lowered himself into the wicker garden chair. Frankie lay down at his feet. He flipped open the cardboard container and sniffed deeply. He picked up a sausage, tore the end off and tossed it to the dog.

"This is the life, eh pal?"

Frankie yipped through a mouthful of sausage. It was more of a high pitched squeak than a bark.

"He'll get fat, you know." Tania put a hand on his shoulder and kissed the top of his head. "Morning Dad."

He patted her hand. "Morning Love."

She fanned three newspapers out in front of his face. "So what's it going to be then? National, sports or local?"

"Local, obviously."

She tilted her head as she handed over *The Occasional Telegraph*. "Why?"

"Because," Liz said as she set the coffees down on the table. "Your father is a morbid sod and likes to read the obituaries on a Sunday morning."

"Wait. You *like* to read the obituaries?"

"When you get to my age it feels like a major achievement to get through a copy of the weekly paper that *doesn't* report on someone you know leaving this mortal coil. You don't understand yet, but you will in time."

Tania scrunched up the corner of her mouth as she sat down with the pink sports paper. She handed the national to Liz and took her coffee.

"Any news on the job front, Tan?" Ernie said as he flicked to the personals near the back of his paper.

"This and that Dad, you know how it is."

"No, I don't."

"Are we really having this conversation again? I've only been here a few hours."

"Listen Love, you can't coast through life, living off my money and hoping the world's going to do you a favour. Life's not like that."

Of course, he recognised her attitude. Tania was him fifty years ago, ducking and diving, running errands and driving for some very dodgy - and dangerous - sorts. He was glad to be well away from that world now. But he was barely out of his teens back then; Tania was almost forty. She needed to take some responsibility.

"Can we lay off the work talk please, Dad? I've got a few things on the horizon and if the right opportunity presents itself, then you won't need to worry about me. Okay?"

"Okay, okay." He held his hands up. "It's just... I do worry about you, that's all," he said through a mouthful of black pudding dipped in runny egg yolk.

"I know Dad." She kissed his hand. "Now eat your breakfast before it gets cold!"

The three read their papers in silence apart from the occasional rustle of pages, slurps and munches, or snuffles from the dog.

After a few minutes, Ernie broke the silence. "Hey, Liz?"

She looked up. He was pressing his index finger down

on the page.

"PLANUS Labs. Ain't that the place you worked when we first met?"

"What?" She put down her coffee. "They usually shut down any news stories long before they get to the printers."

"It's not a story," he said. "It's one of the obits. Listen."

He held up the paper and coughed.

"Robert Smallwood aged 88 years old passed peacefully on the 25th of March after a long illness. A true gentleman who will be missed by Debbie and Tim and all the staff at PLANUS Labs. No flowers please. Donations to The Woodland Trust gratefully received. He loved badgers and badgers loved him."

Tania looked up from her paper. "What does that last bit about badgers mean?"

"Dunno." He took another sip of coffee and turned to Liz. "Do you know who that is?"

"I think so." She scratched her chin. "There was an old gamekeeper. Bert, they called him. Must be the same guy. When PLANUS bought Hawthorne Manor and its grounds back in the sixties, part of the deal was to let him keep his home on the edge of the grounds. He pretty much had free reign of the forest. He was a living stereotype, exactly how you'd expect a gamekeeper to look; all tweed and leather with a big bushy beard, often pottering about the woods and sometimes on the lab's property. He was pretty harmless but he was always on at us to do more to protect the forest and his beloved badgers."

"So did the lab employ him?" Tania said.

"No, not really. It was more of a goodwill thing. His share from the sale of the house was handsome. Set him up for life, I reckon. He was only in his thirties and he probably could have retired there and then. He certainly wasn't required to perform any gamekeeping work after that, but he did anyway. The bosses at PLANUS let him because, to be honest, it was good for business. His constant patrolling kept unwanted elements from snooping around."

"Oh, okay." Tania leaned in and rested her chin on her hand. "So he's not likely to be replaced then?"

"I very much doubt it. Shame really. I spoke to him a few times. Lovely guy." Liz took another sip of her coffee and returned to her paper.

Ernie scanned the personals for any other names he or Liz might recognise. He squeezed a huge dollop of ketchup all over the remains of his fried bread and threw Frankie another piece of sausage.

Tania folded her paper, stood up, drained her coffee and tipped the mug up to show it was empty. "I'm going to make another drink," she said.

Ernie chuckled. "Steady on Love. You'll be bouncing off the walls!"

"I need the caffeine after the long drive," she said with a wink.

She slid the patio door shut with a whoosh as she entered the kitchen. She turned on the kettle and while she waited for it to boil, she slid behind the curtain, checking to make sure nobody in the garden could see what she was doing. She pulled a phone from her pocket and dialled.

"Benny?" she whispered, holding her hand over her mouth. "It's Tan. Listen. This is it! The big score we've talked about. You know how Big Col was looking for some new blood for his games? Well, get yourself and one of the lads up to a town called Badgers Crossing. I think I've found a—"

She paused.

"It's in... oh, never mind. I'll text you directions later. Just acquire a four-by-four - a big one - and get up here. Can you do that?"

Another pause.

"Good. I'll see you in a couple of weeks. Oh, and Benny? Make sure you bring plenty of cages."

WAYFARERS

Now

"Sounds great. We'll talk about it later, okay?"

Click.

Shanice Grant hung up the phone with a snort of disgust.

"Hedgehog? Gross!"

Tyrese and his big sister exploded into giggles.

"Great job Shan," he said, patting her leg. "Your Mum impression is so good, it's scary! I owe you one."

"Yeah, you do. Big time. I was thinking a whole month of my laundry duty–"

"A month! Come on now, be reasonable!" He scratched his head. "How about three weeks?"

Shanice shook her head and laughed. "Done! I would have accepted one, haha! Great negotiation skills, Bruv. Your powers are weak."

Ty clenched his fist. *Damn!*

"If you strike me down, I'll become more powerful than you could ever imagine." It didn't really make sense, but he had to come back with something.

"Whatever you say, small fry." She ruffled his hair as he tried to slap her hand away. "So, what's the plan next, then?"

"If you keep up your end of the bargain–"

"Which I will," she snapped.

"Good. Then when Mum gets home, you tell her that

I've gone to Debbie's for a sleepover and Mr Carter said it was okay. Maybe say he came over to pick me up or something. Don't go mad with details but make something good up. Should be late enough that she won't ring Debbie's house to check."

"Got it. And I suppose you're not going to tell me where you're going tonight?"

"All you need to know is that it's safe, and I'll have my phone with me just in case. I'll ring from the cottage in the morning and tell Mum we're going down the park or something. She'll never even know."

He walked into the kitchen. Shanice followed. He pulled bread down from the cupboard and started to make sandwiches.

His cheese cutting powers were also weak. Some of the slices were thicker than the bread.

She elbowed him in the ribs and said, "I'm taking a big risk, you know? I'll probably get grounded for longer than you will if we get caught."

"I know." He licked butter from the knife.

She screwed up her nose. "This had better be worth it."

"Oh, it is. It's really important. Debbie says so."

"Ooo, Debbie says so," Shanice mimicked.

Her Ty impression wasn't as good as the one of her mum. He shook his head at her.

"I'll bring back some photos, okay?"

He wrapped the sandwiches in foil and stuffed them into his backpack, followed by some chocolate biscuits, a family-sized bag of crisps and a few cans of fizzy pop. He topped this feast off with an apple, not because he particularly wanted one but if he *did* get caught, at least he couldn't be accused of eating unhealthily.

"UTINI!" came a shrill cry from Ty's pocket.

"So lame," she muttered. "Stupid *Star Trek*."

Shaking his head at his sister's ignorance, Ty whipped out his phone and read the text message.

On way!! CU @ meeting point @ 5
DON'T BEE LATE!!

He smiled at the three bumblebee emojis at the end of the message.

"Gotta go!" He fastened his backpack tight and hitched it up onto his elbows. He slid his arms in and fastened the buckle across his chest with a click. Then he dashed into the hallway, grabbing his red and black bicycle helmet on the way and ran out of the door, leaving it wide open as he pulled the helmet over his head.

Shanice followed him to the front garden. "Just promise me one thing, yeah?"

"Er. Okay," he shouted back, wondering what she was going to ask.

"Promise me it's not dangerous, and if you get into any trouble, you'll call me, or Mum, or Tim, or even the police right away, yeah?"

"It's not dangerous." He trotted back to her and rested a hand on her shoulder. "And I promise, I will call if *anything* goes wrong."

He walked back to his mountain bike which was far too big for him, clambered onto it and flicked the pedal up with his foot.

"See you tomorrow night, Sis!" he yelled. He pushed off on the pedal, zooming out of the driveway and down the road before Shanice had a chance to reply.

"I've got a bad feeling about this," she whispered to herself.

***

The setting sun glinted through the trees as Debbie pulled up at the bicycle shelter in the corner of Penlock Forest's car park. After locking her bike to the metal frame, she checked her watch.

17:02

Ty was late.

She pulled her phone out of her back pocket. Out here on the edge of town, the signal was struggling. She held it up above her head, trying to get a better reception pacing back and forth waiting for something to happen.

"Come on, come on," she chanted.

Finally, the voice of Yoda announced "Message from the Dark Side, you have."

"At last!"

Three bumblebee emojis were preceded by the message:

BEE THERE SOON!

"Where are you, Tyrese Grant?"

"Behind you!"

Debbie spun around and pressed her hand into her chest. Ty was locking his bike up next to hers.

She ran over to him and mock-punched him on the arm.

"Idiot!" She said, laughing.

"Ow! What was that for?" he said. It didn't hurt but he still made a point of rubbing his arm, just for show. "So, what's the plan then?"

"Well first," she put one hand on her hip and held her other up with the index finger raised to the sky. "You have to agree to do what I say." She tilted her head to one side. "Got it?"

"Yes, ma'am" he made the Cub Scout salute and grinned.

She ignored this.

"And second, you have to be as quiet as you can. Turn your phone off, or put it on silent in your bag or something–"

"But–"

Debbie pressed her finger to his lips and shook her head.

"Good! You're a fast learner!" She tugged at the rucksack handles over her shoulder and let the pack slide down to her elbows, slipping one arm out, then the other. She placed it on a dustbin and released the walking stick from the straps holding it in place.

Ty did the same. He had one of those fancy hiking poles from the camping shop in town, with a rubber foot, elasticated wrist strap and adjustable length.

Not as good as mine, she thought, running a finger over the carved badger head handle.

The pair of them put their packs back on and Ty made to jog through the gate into the forest. Debbie swung her cane and brought it to rest horizontally over the gate to block his way.

"No," she said, much more sternly than she intended to. Then softening her voice somewhat. "If you want to see a badger this evening then we go slowly, and quietly."

He nodded.

She thumped her chest "And I go first. Okay?"

"Lead the way, your majesty," he said with a smirk.

They left the concrete plaza and stepped through the gate into the shade of the trees. They were only feet away from the road but everything was already quieter.

"Oh, and one more thing. Probably the most important of all." She stopped and turned to face him.

Ty's smile froze in place and ebbed away when he saw the serious look on Debbie's face.

"Do *not* leave the dirt track unless I say. I'm serious."

***

They followed the track for about a mile before Ty spoke again.

"So when do we find these badgers?"

Without turning back Debbie continued, swinging her cane back and forth to part the long grass overhanging from either side of the track.

"Not yet," she said. She stopped and planted her cane in the ground. He almost walked right into her.

"Badgers are nocturnal," she said. That means–"

"They only come out at night, yeah, I know what it means," he said.

"But it's not as simple as that," she said.

"What?" He scratched his head as she set off into the forest again. He followed.

"You see, the clocks have changed and the nights are shorter, but badgers don't wear watches–"

He laughed with a snort.

"So they don't know the clocks have changed, and they have to feed, whether it's dark or not, so they come out at the same time anyway, and the closer to midsummer we get, the more likely we are to see one in the daylight."

Ty nodded at her wisdom and looked at his own watch. "So you think we'll see them around, what? Half eight? Nine?"

"Something like that, just after it gets properly dark."

"So why are we here at five?"

She glanced back over her shoulder. "There's a good reason for all that."

"What's that then?"

"You'll see," she replied and picked up the pace.

Ty knew better than to push Debbie for more information if she wasn't giving any. He followed her in silence, only grunting the occasional affirmation to her when she pointed out obstacles on the path. The setting afternoon sun glistened red and gold through the emerald canopy as they continued deeper into the woods. Birds chirped happily in their treetop homes, the undergrowth was alive with the scurrying of small creatures going about their woodland business and the gentle, warm breeze rustled through the leaves.

"Noisy, innit?" he said.

Debbie shook her head and rolled her eyes. She

stopped at the edge of a steep slope and turned back to him.

"Okay, now do exactly as I do here. We're leaving the path–"

"But you said–"

"I know what I said. It was "Don't leave the path unless I say". And now I say."

Ty wasn't sure if the sun had gone behind a cloud, or if the foliage was just denser here, and even though the breeze had dwindled, it seemed colder.

And darker.

Birds were no longer singing their afternoon chorus and all scurrying in the bushes seemed to have suddenly ceased.

He shivered. Goose-pimples rose on his arms and Ty realised he was going to need his coat. He cursed himself. He hadn't brought it with him. The Weather said it was supposed to be warm for the next few days.

Ahead of him, Debbie began to descend the slope, carefully stepping around the rocks and brambles, using her cane to keep her footing. Ty followed, steadying himself with his own walking pole. As they neared the base of the slope the pair pulled back a branch thick with leaves, revealing a large area of grey rubble. On the ballast were two long strips of rusting metal sitting atop mossy, rotting blocks of wood.

Ty gasped. "This is the railway!"

He tilted his head and squinted at the track to his left as it disappeared into the woods. He turned his head, following the tracks to his right. The slopes at the edge of the track became steeper. Through the weeds and

vines that climbed the now vertical sides, Ty could make
out moss-covered brickwork, walls that cut into the side
of the hill on each side of the track.

Perpendicular to these walls was a vast arch that once
granted passage to and from the wider world. The
tunnel was boarded up with a patchwork of corrugated
metal and chipboard. The entire facade was covered in
graffiti. Some of the words and imagery, he thought,
were really quite artistic and cool but some of it was kind
of creepy and disturbing. Scrawled across the middle of
it all, in red paint, were the words:

BEWARE THE CONDUCTOR

Ty shivered. *Railways Are Not Playgrounds. That's
what The Conductor always says before he takes you,
isn't it?*

An elaborate stone portico surrounded the colourful
canvas. At the very zenith of the arch was a carved
plaque bearing the words:

GRAVELING HILL 1868

"We shouldn't be here," he said.

"We're only crossing the track," Debbie said,
although she too had stopped to stare at the vast portal
to the world beneath Graveling Hill.

"Listen. What's that?" Ty whispered. He cocked his
head and held his hand to his ear. Even though down by
the tracks was sheltered from the breeze a barely audible
whistling began to fill the air. It wasn't a natural sound,
he thought, like when the wind moaned and shrieked

through the caves up in the Whistling Ridge, but more like an actual whistle. Not one with a ball though, like a referee or PE teacher used, but more like an old fashioned policeman's whistle. It was high-pitched and barely audible, but what he could hear hurt his ears.

"Oh, don't worry," Debbie said, waving her hand. "The Conductor isn't real. My dad said so." She scrambled across the rubble up to the blocked entrance. "It's just the wind coming through the tunnel and escaping through gaps in the boards. Look."

She pulled at the edge of a section of the corrugated iron which began to peel away with a loud clattering noise.

The explanation didn't make Ty feel any better.

It didn't sound like wind. It sounded like an old fashioned train guard's whistle.

Debbie poked her head into the hole she'd created.

"Helloo," she called into the blackness. Her voice echoed, drowning out the whistling. When her voice had stopped reverberating the whistle had stopped.

Ty crept along the track towards Debbie. He slowly peered into the hole and immediately leapt back with a cry, losing his footing on the ballast and collapsing to the floor.

"There's somebody in there! I saw them moving!" He clambered to his feet and retreated from the tunnel. Even though he had never been here before and there hadn't been a train since before he had even been born, he still looked both ways before he scrambled up over the ballast and ran to the base of the slope at the other side of the tracks.

"Run!"

Without offering any argument Debbie quickly followed him. They climbed the bank, pushing their way through the bushes and weeds. As they reached the top of the slope the sun came back through the trees, scattering blotches of light over their faces, warming them instantly. The gentle sounds of wildlife began to fill the air again.

The pair looked at each other. They were both hunched over, hands on their knees, gasping for breath after the climb. Without a word, they both burst out laughing.

"Run?" Debbie said through guffaws. "I've never climbed that bank faster. I'm totally zonked out now!"

Ty struggled for air. He gently slapped her on the shoulder.

"Me too."

"There totally wasn't someone in there, you know," she said.

As his breath settled back into its normal rhythm he said, "You're probably right."

However, he didn't believe it. There had been someone in there. He was sure of it.

***

They picked up another path on the other side of the railway and followed it for ten more minutes when Debbie suddenly broke to the left between two huge, gnarled old trees.

"Almost there," she called back. "You any good at long jump?"

"Long jump?" he said as he raised an eyebrow. "Why?"

"Oh nothing really, we just have to get over the Oldbrook. We could go up the side of Graveling Hill and cross it further along. It flows faster there, but there are stepping stones." She pointed to their right, at the steep incline.

"That looks like hard work," he said. "Any other way over?"

"Well, we could go south where the second railway track crosses the river and use the bridge there or we could just head straight on and try to jump over. It's not too far, maybe two metres. About the height of a grown-up."

Ty shuddered as he remembered how cold it had been in the shadow of the tunnel, and that creepy whistling sound. He'd rather not go near any more railway tracks for a good long while.

"You done it before?"

"Loads of times."

"You ever fell in?"

"Loads of times!" she nodded, grinning.

A chuckle escaped his lips as he pictured her sitting in the water, her face a picture of annoyance. It was a look he knew well from the times she'd failed at a task at school or, even worse, he'd done it better.

"Okay then. Let's do it," he said.

She nodded and pulled a clump of overgrown grass aside to reveal a much smaller track through the undergrowth.

Up ahead, Ty could hear the gentle splashing of

running water. He strained through the greenery and could just make out the glisten of the almost set sun as it sparkled like diamonds on the undulating surface of the stream.

Debbie took hold of his hand and gripped it tight. He turned to her to ask what she was doing but before he could speak she cut him off.

"We go together right? We run from here and on three, we jump. Don't think about it, just go, and don't let go, okay?"

He nodded.

"Okay then, here we go!" She started running, dragging him behind her.

"One!"

He pounded at the soil to keep up, laughing as they went.

"Two!"

The last of the scrub parted and the river came fully into view.

That's more than two metres!

"Three! Jump!"

They were going way too fast to stop or slow down so he bent his knees and pushed off from the edge of the river bank with all of his strength, letting out a yell of effort as he left the ground. As the pair sailed in a gentle arc over the water, hand in hand, all he could think of was how if he fell in, his phone would be ruined.

Time seemed to slow as they soared through the air. The river looked motionless, and the last of the sun's rays bouncing from its surface looked so solid Ty thought he could touch them. As they reached the apex of their leap he felt his hand, still grasping hers tightly, being forced up in the air, giving them a little more impetus. He pulled his knees up to his chest, as he'd seen long-jumpers doing on the TV, hoping for a little more lift.

We're not going to make it! he thought as their trajectory shifted in a downwards motion. He felt a punch of panic in his belly as Debbie's hand slipped out of his but before he could call out, he was back on the floor with a thud, rolling in the grass. He landed in a heap at Debbie's feet, who of course had landed perfectly. She held her hand out to him, which he took. As she pulled him to his feet he looked back at the raging torrent they had just leapt over and he couldn't help but laugh. They had cleared the water by a good two or three feet. The river wasn't anywhere near as big as he'd thought it was as they'd burst out of the undergrowth. It was little more than a trickling stream.

"I thought I was going for a swim with the fishes there!"

"Me too," Debbie said, struggling for breath.

Once they'd got their breath back and Ty had dusted himself down she leaned in towards him and placed a hand on his shoulder.

"Ready to keep going?" she said.

"Yeah."

"Good. Because we'll be there in just a minute."

They set off again, Debbie swinging her cane to part branches and grass and Ty ducking out of the way as they sprang back towards him.

They came to a stop in the centre of a circle of large,

ancient trees. The grass in the centre of the clearing was a lot shorter than the rest of the forest like it had been mowed. All around the edge of the circular tree line small metallic objects - buckets he realised when he looked closer - were hanging from metal pegs sticking out of the bark. Debbie approached one of the buckets, lifted its lid and examined its contents. She dipped a finger in, licked it and thought for a second.

He stopped beside her and peered into the bucket. It was filled with a thick, clear liquid which was virtually colourless apart from a subtle hint of yellow. It looked like very weak honey. The peg that the bucket was hung on had a spout at the end, from which the strange liquid was very slowly dripping into the mixture with a satisfying "plop" noise.

"Try it," Debbie said.

"Ew, no! What is it?" He screwed up his nose and mouth.

"Syrup silly. It's nice." She dipped another finger in and sucked the end.

"What kind of syrup? Looks like tree sap to me?" Foamy scum that reminded him of the last remnants of a bubble bath floated on the surface. It didn't look very appetising.

"Sycamore. Don't be a baby, just dip your finger in and *try it!*"

He touched the very tip of his finger to the syrup and slowly raised it to his lips. He poked his tongue out, and gently tapped it with the end of the sticky finger, trying to get as little of the sap in his mouth as possible. A large droplet fell onto the outstretched tongue releasing a sweet, buttery flavour. It reminded him of the toffees his grandad always gave him as the sweetness filled his mouth. The tiny droplet of liquid trickled towards the back of his mouth and down his throat.

"Oh my god. That's amazing!"

Debbie beamed as he reached in for another taste, this time sticking his finger deep in his mouth, making sure every drop was licked off. "Who knew syrup came from trees?"

"Well, duh! Where do you think Maple Syrup comes from, you doofus?" she gently punched his shoulder.

"Er. Canada?" he said with a grin.

She shook her head. "Come on, let's check, see if any of these are full."

"Who does all this?" he asked as they made their way around the circle to the next tree.

"Who do you think?" she said with a grunt as she struggled to prize the lid from another bucket.

"You?" he said.

"Mmm-hmm."

The lid came unstuck with a satisfying slurp and a sickly sweet aroma filled the air. It was almost like the candy floss lady's stall at the fair.

"How do you know how to do all this?"

FOLLOW THE COUNTRY CODE

Two Years Ago

"Take these." Bert hooked a bucket over each of Debbie's arms by the handle. "And these."

He held out a hammer which she took.

"And one last thing."

He dropped a plastic bag full of strange-looking metallic objects and rubber tubes into one of the buckets.

"You okay with all that, young miss?" he said.

She nodded.

"Then off we go!" He hobbled to the door and held it open as she struggled to squeeze past with her load. He closed the door and snatched up the badger-head cane that had been leaning up against the wall in the front porch.

Debbie waited at the bottom of the steps at the end of the garden as Bert slowly made his way towards her. He was getting slower lately, and that worried her.

"Oh, don't wait for me," he called to her. "It's down that path," he pointed to a gap between two birch trees. "About 200 yards. There's a clearing. You won't miss it. Go on, run ahead. A young girl like you needs the exercise."

Despite the instruction, she waited for him. The distinctive stripe in his beard, once as black as the night sky and that made him look a bit like a badger, was flecked with grey. She put the buckets down as he reached the step and held out a hand to help him down. His sandpaper-like hand gripped hers, not quite as tightly as it once did, as he descended the stairs.

"I want to walk with you," she said, taking up her buckets again and falling in beside him as he gingerly stepped onto the uneven path into the woods.

The path twisted here and there, but they stuck strictly to it. Unlike so many visitors to these woods, they knew better than to stray from where the land wanted them to go.

"Don't you have any friends your own age you'd rather be spending time - or hanging out with - as you youngsters say?"

"Well, I have one or two. I suppose Sophia's my best friend. We have sleepovers where we stay up and watch DVDs, draw pictures and eat popcorn. And there's Hannah, although sometimes we fight about who's best at running."

"I hope you make up with her," Bert sighed. "Life's too short to fall out over silly things like that."

"We always do," she said. "Mostly."

"Good, good."

They walked on for a moment, enjoying what Bert called The Silence of The Wood. The kind of silence that's so quiet you notice every leaf rustle in the wind, hear every creature scurry through the undergrowth.

"Not silent at all," she had once said. "Really noisy, in fact."

He had just smiled at her and said "That's the best

kind of silence."

"Any boyfriends? I suppose you're old enough now, aren't you?" he said.

"Ew! No!" Debbie cried. The woodland creatures stopped their scampering for a moment at this outburst and then carried on. "Well, there's one boy. But he's a boy who's my friend, not my boyfriend," she spat the last word as if she'd put something unpalatable in her mouth, like celery or mackerel. "His name is Ty Grant."

"Tie? Like you wear to a wedding?" He chuckled. "That's a funny name and no mistake!"

"It's Ty! Not Tie!" she said, making no attempt to pronounce the two words differently, as though it was obvious. "Tee-Why! It's short for Tyrese."

"That's an interesting name," Bert said.

"He's named after his dad, who died when he was little. His uncle was a famous writer but he disappeared. His grandparents came from Jamaica. "

"Oh, Jamaica, eh? I went there once when I was a young man. Amazing place, so it was. You should bring him or one of your other friends out here one time, I'd love to meet them." He stopped as the path opened out into a wide, circular clearing. The noon sun beating down into the dell through the haze of dust, pollen and insects created a magical glow in the air that reminded Debbie of a cartoon she once saw about King Arthur pulling a sword from an anvil.

"Right, here we are," he said. "Let's get to work."

He walked over to the largest of the trees bordering the clearing. Through its lush canopy, she thought that the trunk and larger boughs made it look like a man reaching out to greet visitors.

"That tree looks like it wants to hug us!" she laughed.

"It does rather!" he agreed. "That, Debbie, is the Walburg Sycamore."

"It has a name?" she said, in awe.

"This one does. She's the biggest and therefore most probably the oldest tree in the forest. Maybe the whole county. Her name, Walburg, means she's a protector." He tapped the gnarled trunk with his badger-cane. "And today she's going to help us."

"She is?"

"You bet, she is."

He walked around the trunk, stopping just out of Debbie's line of sight. She followed him. Near the base, hanging from a metal pipe sticking out of the bough, was a bucket like the one she was carrying. A clear plastic tube ran from the end of the pipe through a hole in the bucket's lid.

"Syrup, Debbie," he pre-empted, seeing the quizzical look on her face.

"Syrup? Like on pancakes?"

"Exactly!" he said. "We're here to harvest it. And these taps have been here a while so we're going to set new ones."

"Taps? Like in the bathroom?"

"Just like in the bathroom," he said. "The taps collect sap - that's like the tree's blood, the fluid that keeps it alive - and we can then use it for all kinds of things,"

She scratched her cheek, and tilted her head, "Doesn't that hurt the tree? Taking its blood?"

"Trees don't feel pain in the same way animals and

people do, but if you do this wrong, then, yes, you could harm it. We're going to remove this tap and open another further round the tree. It's not good for the tree to tap from the same hole all of the time. Don't worry, the holes will heal themselves, and by this time next year, you won't even know where it was."

He removed the bucket from the notch on the end of the pipe, lifted the lid and sniffed at the contents, before setting it down. With a tug, he pulled the plastic tube from the tap. It made a popping noise like Debbie's dad always did with his finger in his cheek. It made her giggle.

"Hand me the hammer please," Bert said. He hooked the claw end around the metal tap and gently pivoted the pipe out of the tree. He wiped it with a handkerchief and dropped it into his pocket with the sticky rag. Thick sap dribbled down the moss-covered bark. He reached into the bag over his shoulder and pulled out an unusual tool. To Debbie, it looked like her dad's hand-powered whisk, but there was a drill bit on the end.

"Now it's your turn," He handed her the drill. "Find a spot, at about waist height. *My* waist height," he laughed as she started to clamber to her knees. "And at least six inches - about a handspan - from the last hole." he held up his hand with the fingers stretched out .

She took the drill. She knew from her dad's equipment in the garage to be careful around power tools so she handled it very tentatively.

"Got your spot?" he asked?

She nodded.

"Good. Now line it up and drill in about two inches.

I've drawn a line on the bit with a marker. Don't go any deeper than that."

She nodded again. Pressing hard against the grip, she began to turn the handle slowly.

"That's it, you've got it. You can speed it up a little. That's it. Good!"

After about two minutes the black line on the bit lined up with the bark, so Debbie stopped and tried to pull the drill out. It was stuck fast.

"Keep turning, slowly, and then ever so gently you can pull it out," he instructed.

She obeyed and the drill came out with ease. A clear liquid began to trickle from the new hole. Bert handed her one of the small metal pipes she had carried.

"Now hammer that into the hole, until you feel resistance," he sensed her about to question that last word. "Until it stops."

She smiled and did as he asked. She stepped back to admire her handiwork as sap began to ooze from her tap.

Bert stepped in and hung one of the new buckets on the notch, took a plastic tube from the bag and ran it from the tap through a hole in the bucket's lid.

"And that's us!" he said.

"How long does that take to fill up? Will it be long?" She said.

"Oh, days. Maybe a week."

"A week? That's ages!"

"Yes it is," he said. "Especially if you've got a sweet tooth like mine."

He winked.

"So do you drill a new hole each time?"

"Oh, no, goodness, no!" he said. "Sycamores produce sap best when it's warm in the day and cold at night. That's only really a small window - three months at best. I put in my taps at Imbolc - the first of February - and remove them for the year on Beltane - or May Day if you like. Occasionally, like today, I put in new taps, but not always. Only if the weather's playing up and the tap I've sunk is not bearing much syrup."

"This one here," he gently kicked at one of the full buckets. "Was just about spent, I reckon." The thick liquid sloshed around. "But never mind that now. We've got more to do. Come on."

Over the next hour, they repeated the process on three more of the trees in the circle, until all the empty buckets were used up.

"And now," he said, packing the used, sticky parts into a plastic carrier bag that he'd stuffed into his shoulder bag with the drill and hammer, "the fun part!"

He picked up one of the buckets in one hand, and firmly grasped his cane in the other. Debbie wrestled with the other three as the pair made their way back along the short trail to Bert's house.

"So we eat it, right?" she said eagerly.

"Well, it is edible immediately," he said. "But it's better to cook it. Gets rid of impurities and intensifies - that's 'makes stronger' - the sweetness."

"And then we eat it?"

He chuckled. "And then we eat it," he said with a nod. "But not all of it. Let's save some for our friends, yes?"

She knew exactly what that meant. The badgers. No

matter how many times she stayed over at Bert's, she never, ever tired of them coming over for their dinner. Each night two, sometimes three or even four of the creatures shuffled up to his porch, where he laid on a veritable banquet for them, made up of all kinds of goodies from the forest, and one or two treats from the supermarket. But tonight those lucky badgers were getting syrup!

When they were almost back to the house Bert stopped for a second, his breathing heavier than usual. She looked up to him, her face full of concern.

"Don't worry," he said through gasps, "I'm just tired. It gets harder each time. I'm just getting old. I'm glad you were here to help me. One day, when I'm no longer here, then maybe you can do this all by yourself, or with one of those friends of yours."

She winced at the sting of tears in the corner of her eye, brought on by the thought of him not being in her life anymore.

"These trees have been feeding the forest since long before I was here and they will be for a long time after I've gone."

Now

"This is the third harvest that I've done now." Debbie sighed. "But the first time ever without Bert." She slumped down on a mossy tree stump that Bert had made a bench from by nailing a few planks to it.

Ty sat beside her, not sure what to say.

"I'm glad you were here to help me today, Ty."

"Yeah, me too." He smiled.

"Come on." She leapt up and patted one of the buckets, which responded with a sloshing sound. "Let's take these back."

"Back where?" he said as he pushed himself up.

"You'll see." She winked at him, and traipsed up the overgrown trail alongside the Walburg Sycamore, being careful not to spill too much of the syrup as she went.

PART 2: MORITASGUS AMBULAT

DARK TOWERS

"Oh. My. God!" Ty said with a gasp when the house came fully into view. At first glance, through the wood, it looked like a fairly normal cottage, typical of many of the houses in Penlock village or the older parts of Badgers Crossing. What had surprised him, though, was the other half of the house that had been hidden by the trees until now.

He stared up, mouth gaping at the great stone turret towering over the rest of the cottage, which it was more than twice the height of.

"Bert lived in a castle?" he said.

Debbie giggled. "Not quite! It's called a folly. He told me that the people up at Hawthorne Manor built it hundreds of years ago for no other reason than to show off their money. Before the forest grew all over this hill every single one of their neighbours could see it, and it made them jealous."

"So how did Bert end up in it?"

"Over the years, a cottage was built on the side of it and because it was near the edge of the woods, it became the gamekeeper's lodge. Bert was the last gamekeeper before the manor was bought by that science place. They had no use for it so it was given to him as part of his reduce... redunt... REDUNDANCY! package."

"Whoah! It's so cool."

"Yes it is," she said with a smirk. "And now it's mine."

"It's... it's yours?" Ty's jaw dropped again. She

pushed his chin back up.

"You mustn't tell anyone." She eyed him suspiciously. "Promise me."

"Er, okay. Why not?"

"I'm supposed to get it when I'm eighteen, but that's like forever in the future, and it's being looked after by some people until then, but they only come out here once a month to clean it and check on it. My dad and me stayed out here for a night, to clear it out and stuff last weekend, but when I went to see Bert in the hospital just before he died he gave me a secret mission. Check this out."

She opened the head of the badger cane as Bert had shown her and produced the shimmering key.

"Woah! Sleepover! With no grown-ups! Excellent!"

With a smirk, Debbie winked at him.

"I know."

***

After a quick toilet break, Debbie showed Ty how to preserve the syrup by filtering, double boiling and bottling it. She put the still-hot glass bottles they'd worked on in a store cupboard and held out a fresh, cool one from a shelf full of them.

"Put this in your bag. We'll need it tonight."

He took the bottle. Then she handed him a tin bowl, like the sort he used to eat his breakfast cereal from on Scout camp.

"What's this for?" he called as he walked into the lounge and unzipped his backpack. "We're not going to drink it, are we?"

"No! We're going to feed it to the badgers. Bert always used to say that if you reward them, they'll reward you. I didn't understand what that meant at first, but then one time I was lost in the woods and I gave a badger some crisps and it showed me the way out."

Ty emptied his snacks and clothes from his backpack onto the sofa-bed and shoved the bowl and the bottle in, making sure it was the right way up. If that stuff leaked he'd never get it out. Then he pulled a charging plug out and held it up.

"Can I plug this in?" he said. "I'm almost down to zero."

"Yeah, down there." She pointed to a wall socket beside the ancient-looking tube television. "You might as well leave your phone here tonight anyway. I am. No signal out in the woods."

He nodded and plugged his phone in. It lit up the room as the charging icon informed him there was only 9% battery life left.

"What about Wi-Fi?" he said, flicking to the Wireless Network settings screen.

"Yeah, you can join it if you want."

He scrolled through several wireless networks with PLANUS_LABS in the title - *that must be the science place Debbie mentioned*, he thought - until he came to a network called BERT_COTTAGE. *This must be it.*

"Password?" he called out to Debbie, who was still fussing around in the kitchen, clanking bottles.

"It's on the fireplace. All caps, underscore between the words, yeah?"

He looked up at the stone lintel. Two words he did

not recognise were neatly carved into it:

MORITASGUS AMBULAT

He tapped the password into the phone and, once he was satisfied it had joined the internet - heralded by an array of bleeps, pings and UTINI!s - he locked the screen and walked back to the kitchen. He hadn't realised how dark it had got until he noticed that he was feeling his way along the wall in the gloom.

"What does it mean?" he said as he entered the kitchen.

"What does what mean?"

"Morty Sang Us Ambulance."

Debbie burst out laughing at his mangled pronunciation.

"Moritasgus Ambulat," she said through titters.

"Yeah, that." The heat of embarrassment prickled his cheeks.

"It means Moritasgus Walks. And before you ask, Moritasgus is a woodland god of healing, from ancient times. He was like half-man, half-badger - it literally means 'The Great Badger'."

"The Great Badger Walks? What's that mean then?"

"Well you know how church people like Reverend Pierce say that Jesus is still alive today?" she said.

He nodded. He knew it well. He'd been to plenty of Sunday School lessons at St Piran's. His mum was in the choir.

"Well, I think Bert believed that this Moritasgus was still alive and lived in the woods, right here, healing sick creatures, helping lost travellers, protecting the forest and stuff."

Ty snorted. "Yeah, right!"

Debbie slapped his arm. "It's not nice to make fun of people's beliefs, even if you think they're silly."

He bowed his head and muttered "Sorry," under his breath.

"It's okay," she said, rubbing the spot where she'd hit him. "I didn't believe it when I heard it either."

"And do you now?" he said.

"I'm not sure what I believe. Sometimes I feel like the forest is looking out for me, and other times I feel like it really doesn't want me there. One thing's for sure though; I've never seen a giant werebadger walking about the place!"

The idea of a werebadger made the pair of them explode into gales of laughter. When they'd regained their composure, Debbie held up some of the bottles of syrup they'd made.

"We'll put these in the big freezer in the garage and then go, yeah?"

***

Debbie froze as they made their way around to the front of the house. "What on earth?"

"What's up?" Ty said.

She pointed at the Land Rover blocking the front of the garage door.

"I thought the solicitor had sold Bert's car. Well, I guess I was wrong. I'll never get the garage door open with that there! Stupid! Wait here, I'll go and put these in the freezer in the house for now. Just a minute."

She headed back around the house. Once she was out of sight Ty felt the flesh in the back of his neck creeping with goose pimples. It was colder out here now the sun had gone down, but not *that* cold. He'd never been out in the woods, on his own, in the dark before. It wasn't exactly silent, but the night-time sounds of the woodland were very different to those in the day. The only rustling now was the occasional breeze through the treetops. The spring canopy was not fully grown yet and some of the bare branches rattled together like the bamboo wind chimes his mum had in the garden.

He shivered as the shriek of a fox in the distance pierced the darkness. It was a sound he was familiar with, living in a small country town, but no matter how many times he heard it he still always imagined a person screaming out in terror. With his senses on edge, he listened closely for anything that might be creeping up on him from the darkness. That was when he heard the other sounds.

At first, it was the barking - high pitched and grumpy. He dismissed it as guard dogs at the science place that he knew was just a short distance behind the trees at the front of the house. But it sounded like a small dog, and high-security places didn't use Jack Russells, did they?

As he strained to hear beyond the barking and the click-clack of the trees he could also make out voices. He couldn't tell what they were saying, or how many of them there were, but there were definitely a few of them. Adults; both men and women, and they were talking, not shouting. They weren't very far away at all.

"Okay, let's go!" Debbie clapped a hand down on his

shoulder.

Ty made a noise that he was embarrassed to realise sounded a lot like the call of the fox he'd heard. Except where the creature had made an inhuman shriek, he had bellowed a word he knew he would get grounded for even thinking, never mind shouting out loud.

As the echoes of his yell faded away he realised that the nearby voices had all stopped. All except the crotchety dog, whose irascible yaps now sounded a lot louder. And closer.

It was coming this way.

And one of the voices started again, following it.

"Reggie! Come back! Reggie!"

PROTECT AND SURVIVE

"What the hell was that?" Will Sampson whispered. He glanced over his shoulder in the direction that the unearthly, almost human sounding howl had come from.

"Just a fox," said Tania. "Nothing to be scared of, you big baby."

"It sounded so human, almost like it said–"

"We all heard it. It was very amusing. See how much it made me laugh." She glared at him. "It's just the mating cry of a female fox. We'll hear plenty more before we're done here. Get used to it."

"I don't like it," he said. "I feel like I'm being watched."

"We are being watched," she said. "Every single thing out here has its beady eye on us, keeping their distance. You just learn to ignore it. They won't hurt you."

Will glanced at the stack of wire cages. Tania was right. A mass of small eyes, glowing in the moonlight peered at him silently from the blackness behind the bars, following his every move. He shivered and turned away from their unshakeable stare.

Reggie the dachshund was also perturbed by the shriek. He tugged at his leash in the direction of the sound, yelping angrily.

"Benny, keep that bloody animal under control," Tania hissed at her other companion.

Labhesh Bendra struggled to hold onto the

squirming dog but Reggie had other ideas. He wriggled free of his master's grasp and scampered off into the woods towards the source of the noise, leash trailing behind him.

"Reggie! Come back! Reggie!"

"Christ, Benny!" Tania said. She grasped a clump of her hair in frustration. "Go and get him!"

Benny flicked on his torch and hurtled into the woods, calling after his troublesome dog.

***

Debbie led the way as they fled through the woods. "Step where I step. We'll try to be as quiet as we can. Watch out for that!" She leapt over a protruding root and Ty copied her.

"Who are they?" he said through breathless pants.

"I don't know, but I do know that the visitors' car park is locked up at night, and there are no other houses out here. They're not here for a nice stroll."

"There was a lady's voice. She sounded angry."

"Yeah." Debbie slowed to a jog, and then stopped altogether. "Let's hang on here a minute."

She tiptoed into an area hidden from the path and leaned on a fallen tree to catch her breath. Ty followed, checking the path in both directions for torchlight flickering through the branches before clambering into the bushes with her.

"Nobody's coming," he whispered. "I think."

"Good." She leaned towards him, looking both ways to check herself, not because she didn't believe him but out of instinct. "We need to find out who they are and why they're here."

"What do you mean?" Ty cried, covering his mouth with his hand when he realised how loudly that had come out. "What do you mean?" he said again, in a whisper. "We need to get the hell out of here."

He turned to Debbie who was shaking her head.

"No. I promised Bert I'd look after this place and I'm going to do just that, with or without you. So tell me Ty, are you with or without me?"

He sighed.

"I'm with you. Of course I am. I wouldn't leave you alone out here with strangers. But what are we going to do?"

"Well let's see if we can find out what they're up to first. Come on." She peered out of their hiding place. Still no sign of the man with the torch. The little dog barked somewhere, a long way off in the distance. "Good. They're not following us."

She stepped out onto the path, holding a branch aside for Ty, who climbed out after her.

"Now, remember how I said don't stray from the path? Well we're going to stray from the path. Do exactly what I say and what I do, right?"

He nodded. Seemed sensible. They'd be spotted easily on the path. Debbie unhooked her walking stick from her backpack. Ty reached back for his own to find it was gone. *Damn, I must have left it in the house,* he thought as they entered the undergrowth.

***

"Got him," Benny said as he returned with the dog,

who was pulling and struggling against his leash. "Found him sniffing around back at the car. I also found this." He held up an aluminium hiking pole.

"Let's see," Tania swiped it from his hand and examined it while Benny tied Reggie's lead to a tree.

"Bloody hell, there's somebody out here. We'll get caught," Will said, through fingernails jammed between his teeth.

"I'm not so sure." She held it out to him. "Look."

He took it and turned it over in his hands. After a moment he said "Okay, apart from the fact that it was bought in Outdoor Warehouse, what am I looking for exactly?"

"Try using it," she said.

He unclipped the latch on the side and lengthened it. After he'd snapped it shut again he grasped the hand grip and planted the rubber ferrule end firmly into the hard soil.

"Seems fine to me," he said, leaning into it to see how much weight it could take.

"I'm surrounded by idiots," Tania whispered to herself, rubbing her temple. She tilted her head towards Will. "You just made it a foot longer."

"Yeah, otherwise it'd be way too short for me."

"Kids, Will," said Benny. "There are kids out here."

Will formed a perfect O with his mouth as the penny dropped. He turned to Tania. "I thought you said there was nobody living out here anymore."

"There isn't. Or there shouldn't be."

"So what are we going to do?" Will said.

Benny crouched down, picked up a spade from the

ground and slammed the flat of the blade into his hand.

"We're going to find them and shut them up before they cause us any trouble," he said.

"But... They're children," said Will.

"Do you think Big Col is going to care about that if we come back empty handed?" She cuffed him on the back of his head. As Will protested and rubbed his stinging scalp she unclipped a torch from her belt and flicked it on.

"Let's split up, get out there and bloody well find them!"

***

"I don't like it here," Ty whispered as they tentatively climbed across a patch of ragged brambles, being careful not to get jabbed.

"Yeah, I know. You keep saying," Debbie said.

"I don't mean in the woods, I mean right here, where we are, right now."

"In the thorn bush? It's not exactly my favourite place either."

"No," he stopped to face her. "I mean here, where we are right now." He waved his hand to the woods in general. "Since we left the path."

"Ah, okay. Yeah. There is a reason for that but you're probably not gonna like it." She crouched down and beckoned him to do the same beside her.

"Some people can tell when places are bad. Bert could and me too. Looks like you can as well."

"What do you mean by 'bad'?" he said.

"It's difficult to say."

"Try. Please."

"Well, sometimes something might have died there. There might be a predator. Maybe there's pollution or some other danger. Or it could be a special or evil place we're just not supposed to be. But yeah, now you say it, this place is not good."

She rubbed at her bare arms and the back of her neck which were tingling.

"Let's keep moving," she said. At the thought of something having died here, Ty was happy to comply.

"The animals can tell too. Did you wonder why the paths through the wood are so twisty?"

He shook his head as they clambered through a hollow log.

"Well, they avoid these places, find a way round. Sometimes it's not the quickest way, but they can tell which is the safest. After years they wear away the grass and make the paths. Bert called them Grey Paths and he used to say that they led you where the land wanted you to go."

"I think I understand," he said. "So why are we going where the land doesn't want us to go?"

"It's either that or bump into those people."

"Point taken."

"We're almost there, I think. I can hear that dog whining. That's funny..."

"What?"

"Well, this is near where I was going to bring you tonight anyway. Where the badgers live."

"Do you think these people have come to see them too?" Ty said.

"No. I don't think so. You don't shine torches all over the place, you don't shout your head off, you don't bring a dog with you..." she parted the bushes opposite where she knew the main sett entrance emerged, peered through and gasped. "And you definitely don't bring a load of cages."

***

Will's mind was alive with worry as he traipsed along the trail, flashing his torch back and forth.

Why do I let Tania bully me? Just because her dad was once some big shot bank robber, doesn't give her the right to order us about and hit us.

He rubbed at his tender head that still stung from the slap she had given him.

I've about had enough. One last job. Yeah, one last job and then I'm out. I never signed up for creeping about the woods in the dead of night, freezing my arse off, getting intimidated by... God knows what.

He stopped dead as another banshee shriek from the depths of hell echoed across the wood.

"Christ," he said. At this point he wasn't sure if that was a blasphemous exclamation or a plea for salvation. A bit of both, perhaps.

And God help me, hurting children. That's not something I want to be a part of.

Another scream, much closer this time. He dropped his torch as he thrust both hands to shield his ears from the piercing wail.

It's just in the bushes to my right.

It was followed by a different noise, a quieter but no

less human sounding chattering response from the bushes on his left. He flicked his head in the direction of a noise from the tree tops that sounded like it was calling out "Will! Will!" and spun around when from behind him he heard a response that he could have sworn was a long, drawn out "You. You. YOU!"

Bloody hell, they're all around me. The sooner I'm out of this place the better.

The bushes to his right rustled and shook as he crouched down to pick up his torch. At the sound of something grunting and sniffing, he leapt up and away from greenery.

I'll find those kids and chase them off. Just give them a bit of scare, a thrilling tale to tell their mates at school, nothing more. They'd be damn fools to come back after that. Nobody will get hurt and we'll be out of here before sunrise. After that, I'm telling Tania that I'm done.

"Yeah," he whispered.

With a more determined stride in his step and a plan of action Will set off into the woods.

***

Once Benny had vanished into the darkness, pulled along by the eager dachshund, Tania made her way back to the house. She unlocked the Land Rover, climbed into the passenger seat and pulled her phone out.

Still no reception. She wound down the window and waved the phone about, keeping a close eye on the signal bars.

Nothing.

"Damn. Col will have to wait for his update," she said.

She flipped the car's glove box open and pulled out a small package wrapped in a greasy old tea towel. With her nose turned up at the stinking rag, she peeled the corners back. Once the towel had been unravelled she held the gun up to the moonlight, slid the magazine out of the handle to check it was loaded and when she was satisfied, she slammed it back in with her palm.

"Right," she said as she stepped out of the car. "Let's finish this."

***

Debbie and Ty snuck from the bushes, taking care not to step on any twigs or leaves that might give them away.

It feels very uneven.

She looked to the ground. Even in the dark of night she could tell it was a lot messier than the last time she had been here.

"Ty," she whispered, pointing to the floor. "Look."

"Looks like it's been all dug up," he said.

Debbie nodded and then tipped her head towards the cages.

"Come on."

They crept across the moonlit clearing, listening carefully for the approach of the adults who they were painfully aware were out there *somewhere.*

As they tiptoed to the other side of the glade, moonlight glinted and flashed off the cages. They crept back into the shadows and Debbie struggled to hold back a sob. It wasn't the cages reflecting the moon's rays. It was eyes. Several pairs of tiny black eyes, staring back at her.

She pressed her hand to the wire frame of the nearest cage and felt the tingle of a cold wet nose press against her palm.

"Badgers?" Ty said.

In her distress she had forgotten he was there. She nodded grimly.

"This is Monty. He was born just two months ago." She pointed to the cage stacked above it. "Sarah, his sister," and another "Percy, another from the litter." A tear trickled down her cheek. "What have they done to you?"

From her left she heard a hiss. She whipped her head around to see Ty crouching and reaching out towards one of the ground level cages. The creature inside was baring its fangs. Its shoulder muscles were tensed and pushed forward to make it look twice as big.

"No!" she cried as quietly as she could. "They don't know you. They don't trust you yet."

He pulled his hand away from a cage.

"But–"

"I said no! If you reward them, they'll reward you, remember?"

Ty thought about this for a second as realisation crept across his face.

"Oh!" He slid his backpack down from his shoulders, unzipped it and pulled out the bottle of syrup and the tin bowl. He unscrewed the lid and poured a small amount into the bowl. He turned to Debbie. She nodded, as if to say "That's right. Go on."

Very slowly he slid the bowl across the floor to the

cage. It didn't quite fit through the mesh, but he was able to push some of it into the enclosure. Without taking his eye off the badger, he slowly pulled his hand away. At first it continued its show of strength, but when it was satisfied that Ty was not a threat, it lowered its shoulders, shrinking itself down to a size similar to the other creatures around it. Keeping its teeth on display, the badger tentatively padded forward, never taking its eyes off Ty. It sniffed the air above the bowl and gave Ty one last look before relaxing its lips.

With its fangs out it was a vision of terror, Ty thought. With them safely tucked away it looked like a cuddly toy. How could one animal be so threatening and then so cute?

The badger buried its nose into the corner of the bowl that protruded into the cage and with a lot of slurping and snuffling, it began to lick up the sticky sweet liquid. When it had finished as much of the syrup as it could reach through the bars it slinked back into the corner of its cage with a small nod of the head, as if to say "Thank you". Ty shook the remains of the syrup from the bowl, put it back into his bag and fastened it over his shoulders.

"That was Hattie. She's the mother of the cubs," said Debbie.

"How can you tell the difference?"

"Well, males' faces are wider and rounder and their tails are normally white. Females are thinner but have fatter tails which are often black."

"But how can you tell which one is which?" Ty said.

"How can you tell which humans are which?" Debbie

said.

"Well everyone looks different."

"And every badger looks different once you know them. Clint," she pointed to a very fat badger in one of the lower cages, "is always in fights. He has a piece of his ear missing. Regina has what's called erythrism which means her face stripes are red instead of black. Lancelot has a pink spot on his nose and Bert..." she paused. "Bert? Where's Bert?"

"Bert?" Ty said. "Like the old man?"

"Yeah. Bert - my Bert - had a black stripe in his beard. And one side of Bert the badger's face was totally white, no stripe at all. I thought they looked like each other."

"I can see why," he said.

Debbie scanned the cages, counting them with her finger as she went.

"There's only twenty-six here. With the new cubs, there should be twenty-seven." She wiped the tear from her chin. "We have to find him, but let's get these cages open first."

Ty gently reached out to the door of Hattie's cage and tugged at it with a grunt.

"I can't open it, look." A padlock was fastened around the door's catch.

Debbie tugged and pulled at another the cage doors. It was stuck fast and the cage itself was too strong to break or bend the bars.

"No! It's not fair! We have to free them!" she said, spitting with fury, forgetting that she had been trying to keep her voice down.

"We need to find a tool. Pliers or wire cutters or

something."

"Yes! Let's get back to Bert's, see if he's got a–"

Her words were forcibly stopped as the collar of her t-shirt tightened under her chin and she found herself being jerked from her feet.

"You ain't going nowhere, Missy," hissed a voice into her ear.

"Get off me!" she squeaked, struggling to make any noise through her constricted throat. She lashed out, swinging her fists and legs wildly but nothing connected. From the corner of her vision she could see Ty punching the man in the side with no effect.

"Will! Tan!" the man shouted. "Get back to the traps. Now! I've got them!"

"Ty!" she rasped.

He flicked his eyes towards her without stopping his assault. The man, who was fending Ty's attacks off easily, tried to grasp his collar. But Ty was too fast.

"Come here, you slippery little runt," cried the man as Ty dodged his grasping hand.

"Run," Debbie croaked.

"No!" he said through tears of frustration as he continued to pound the seemingly impenetrable man's torso.

"You have to," she whispered. "Get help."

"No! I won't leave you!"

She summoned up every last gasp of air she could.

"RUN!"

Ty leapt back at the sudden ferocity of her cry. The man reached out for the hood of his sweater, but he ducked away from his grip.

The last thing Debbie saw, before everything went black, was her friend disappearing into the bushes.

SCOUT'S HONOUR

Wiping tears from his eyes and blowing snot from his nose, Ty fled into the forest. He could hear voices behind him.

"There's another one!" said the man who had caught Debbie. "He's black. Blue hoodie. A bit taller and wirier than this one. He went that way."

"You," came a woman's voice. "Get after him. Now! And you? Tie her up."

"Get back here!" The third voice, a younger man, was close behind him. The air erupted with the rustling of leaves and cracking of branches.

Ty looked over his shoulder to see the whole forest waving and convulsing. The man was close. He picked up his pace, struggling to divide his concentration between the maze of tree trunks ahead of him, the undulating forest floor and his pursuer. He burst through the trees into a moonlit dell, almost losing his footing on the short grass of the flat clearing because he was expecting it to be uneven underfoot. He quickly glanced around for an escape route when he felt a stab of familiarity.

I know where I am, he thought as he gazed up open mouthed at the enormous Walburg Sycamore ahead of him. *This is where the syrup taps are! I can follow the path all the way back to the river from here.*

He pelted across the clearing towards the trail leading to safety just as the man launched himself out of the trees.

"There you are!"

He obviously wasn't being as careful as Ty had because his knees buckled beneath him when he encountered the sudden change in the relief. He collapsed to the floor with a loud "Oof!".

Ty took the opportunity to sprint back into the trees, taking the path they had arrived by.

"I see you!" called the voice behind him. "You can't escape."

He took the opportunity to look over his shoulder again. The man was on his feet again, but the fall had shaken him. He was quite a way back now and falling further behind.

"Keep going, keep going," Ty chanted to himself. The mantra seemed to calm him as he sped along the Grey Path, focusing his mind and sharpening his senses. He was surprised to find that he was predicting and tackling obstacles quickly, knowing when to take sudden turns, which forks to take and which areas to avoid.

Another look back. The man was still there, but at this rate he would lose him by the time he reached–

"Oh crap! The river!" Ty burst out of the bushes as the rushing water came into view. At night it seemed faster, louder and angrier. With no time to stop for a run up, as they'd done earlier - *was that really just a few hours ago? It feels like days* - he pushed off from the edge of the river bank.

I'll never make it. Not on my own he thought as the spitting, bubbling river came closer and closer. He braced himself for the shock of immersion, ready to swim, to fight the torrent. He closed his eyes. Instead of the surface giving way, parting as he plunged in, it was solid; a landing he hadn't shaped his body for. He felt his left foot twist from under him, bending in a direction he instinctively knew it wasn't supposed to. As he spun over towards the soil, electric sparks of pain shot up his leg from his ankle. His cry was cut short as he landed hard on his chest, forcing all the air from his lungs.

And he knew the man would be upon him imminently.

Fighting the aches in every part of his body, he flipped himself over onto his side and tilted his head forward. Between his feet, one of which was pointing far too much in the wrong direction, he saw the bushes shake as the man exploded onto the river bank.

He saw the look of panic on the man's face as he realised what was in front of him and he saw the man trip and fall face down into the rushing water. It was only half a metre or so deep. It would only be a matter of seconds before the man recovered, climbed to his feet and caught him.

Except the man wasn't getting up. He was lying face down in the water.

Ty pushed himself up against a rock and tentatively put a little weight on his injured foot.

It was no worse than sprains and strains he'd got playing football but he still cried out as those sparks ignited the pain in his ankle again. At least it wasn't broken.

I can make it, he thought. *I can limp the rest of the way.*

He looked back at the river. The man was still face down. He began to hobble away but after two excruciating steps he stopped and turned his head again.

The tingle in his neck and fingers and the falling sensation in his stomach, which, from all the times he'd been caught misbehaving, he recognised as guilt overshadowed the pain in his foot.

"Shit," he said as he limped back to the river.

He clambered down the bank and gasped as the cold water flowed up around his ankles. It actually took his mind off the sprain. He waded the few feet out to the man and tugged at his gilet. He was heavy, but with a mighty heave Ty was able to drag him away from the centre of the stream and turn him over onto his back on the shale bank.

The man had a cut on his forehead and blood flowed down his face.

"Please don't be dead," Ty whispered to him. Thinking back to the first aid badge that he'd earned at Scouts, he started performing CPR. Although Ty wasn't very strong, water spluttered from the man's mouth with each chest compression.

"Thirty presses, two kisses," he recited as the advice the nurse had given to a room full of giggling children came back to him. "Thirty presses, two kisses."

Once he'd reached the required thirty compressions he recalled what they'd done with Annie, the resuscitation dummy. He reached out to pinch the man's nose shut ready to deliver the two breaths of life-giving air.

The man's eyes flew open and his hand shot up, grasping Ty by the wrist. He coughed up another mouthful of dirty river water. His other hand grasped Ty behind the neck and he pulled him close to his face. Ty's breathing became rapid and shallow with fear as the man pulled him so close he could smell the fetid river water on his breath.

"Run," the man gasped, globs of spittle, water and soil splashing Ty's face.

"What?" Ty said.

"Run," the man wheezed. "Get out of here kid. Go now. Before the others get here."

"But are you going to be—"

"I'll be alright. But you won't if they catch you. Now scram!"

Ty pulled himself up the bank with handfuls of grass and climbed to his feet. Perhaps it was the adrenaline, maybe the numbing effect of the freezing river, but the pain in his ankle was nowhere near as bad as it had been.

He hopped away from the river, increasing his speed to an uneven jog and turned back one last time before the river was out of sight. The man was mopping the blood on his head with his palm. With his other hand he waved Ty away.

SAY NO TO STRANGERS

"Kid?"

Darkness. Pain.

"Hey, kid. Wake up!"

Debbie's eyes flew open as a thousand freezing needles pricked at her forehead. She tried to gasp as the icy water ran down her face, neck and back but she struggled to suck in the air. She tried to reach up to her face to remove the thing covering her mouth but her hands appeared to be stuck behind her back.

A man was leaning in towards her. He tilted his head to examine her.

It was the same man from before. The one that had grabbed her. She tried to kick him but her legs were stuck together. She looked to her feet to see what was wrong. A strip of thin plastic, like Dad had used to tidy up the wires behind the telly was fastened around her ankles.

She tried to cry out but all that came out was a muffled "Hurmph" sound. She tilted her eyes downward to see a dirty piece of cloth over her mouth and nose. The rag felt slimy and the sharp smell emitting from it, petrol she thought, made her eyes water.

She wriggled and squirmed, trying to shake free from her restraints.

"She'll be alright," the man said to someone who was standing behind him.

The other person stepped out of the shadows. It was

a woman with long black hair. Her hands were planted into the pockets of one of those waterproof wax jackets like she and Bert sometimes put on when collecting syrup or feeding the badgers in the rain.

"Good," the woman said. "What about Will?"

"Took a nasty bang to the head. Probably a concussion. Might need stitches but he'll live. He'll be no use for a while though."

The woman clenched a fist and nodded.

"Let's see what she knows." She reached out to remove the rag but Debbie turned her head away.

"Hold her still, will you Benny," she said.

The man grasped her by the cheeks with one enormous, strong hand. Debbie tried to scream, shout, spit at him, but the gag prevented her from doing all of that. She tried to wriggle from his grasp but he was too strong and she couldn't shake herself free.

The woman leaned in close and locked eyes with her.

"I'm going to take this off now. There's no point screaming or shouting or trying to call out for anyone. I think you know as well as I do that there's nobody else out here to hear it and you'd be wasting your breath. Do you understand?"

Debbie stopped squirming, tipped her head in a motion that was barely a nod and glared at the woman with a look that seemed to say "I understand, but I don't like it. And I don't like you."

The woman pulled at the knotted fabric behind Debbie's head and it fell away. Debbie sucked in a great gasp of air through her mouth. It burned worse than the time Sophia's big sisters made her, Ty, Olivia and Sophia play Jelly Shot Roulette with them and she'd got the one with the vodka in it.

"What are you doing here?" she spat, partly out of anger but mostly to rid her mouth of the foul oily taste left by the rag.

"What am *I* doing here?" the woman said, surprised. "What are *you* doing here? That's what I want to know."

"These are my woods," Debbie screamed in her face. She didn't care that it made the burning in her throat worse.

The woman wiped away saliva from her cheeks. "Not tonight. I think you'll find these woods, and everything in them, belong to me." She reached into her pocket, pulled out a silver-coloured object and held it up so Debbie could see. "You know what this is?" the woman said.

"I'm ten. I'm not stupid," Debbie said. She'd never seen a gun before, not in real life. Only in those silly action films Dad liked. It was smaller than she expected.

"Well then, you know that I'm serious. So, I'm going to ask you a second time; there won't be a third. What are you doing out here?"

"I already told you. These are my woods and it's my job to look after them."

"You?" The woman laughed. "Well, you're doing a bang up job so far, aren't you?"

That stung. Tears welled in Debbie's eyes.

The woman reached in behind Debbie's back and slid the walking stick out from its loop on the backpack. She turned it over in her hands, admiring it.

"Give that back!" Debbie said. "That's mine."

"Wrong," the woman said. "It's mine now."

More tears. Debbie tried to force them away but she couldn't stop them. Water streamed down her cheeks, but she wasn't going to give the woman the satisfaction of hearing her whimper like a baby. It made the back of her throat ache but she managed to hold the sobs back.

"Oh there, there," the woman continued. "Don't cry." She lifted the filthy rag to Debbie's face and wiped the tear from her cheeks. It left greasy marks on her face. It felt horrid.

She thinned her lips and eyes. Behind her back she clenched her fists.

"You won't get away with this," she said. "My friend will come back and he'll bring help. The police!"

"Ah, yes," said the woman. "This friend of yours. What was his name?"

"I'm not telling you!"

"Tell her what you did to her friend, Will," said the woman.

Debbie's stomach lurched at this.

A third man she hadn't seen before was sitting up against a tree, holding a cloth to his head. Even in the black of night she could see that it was soaked in blood.

"I took care of him, Tania," Will groaned. "Last I saw, he was hurt bad. He won't get far."

Debbie relaxed her hands and feet as the fight went right out of her.

"Ty?"

"So it's Ty, is it?" She turned to the other man. "Benny, take Reggie, get out there and find him."

So now I know all their names, Debbie thought. *Will*

is the young one with the cut on his head, the big Asian man with the moustache, that's Benny. His dog is Reggie and the woman? She's called Tania. She's in charge, I think.

"You'll never find him," Debbie called to Benny as he disappeared into the woods.

Please God, don't let Benny find him.

"Can't we just pack up and leave?" said Will. "We've got what we came for."

"No!" Tania said. "We have to find that kid. And I'm not leaving without that big Alpha that got away, the one with the white face."

Bert escaped!

"Badger clans don't normally have alphas, stupid!" Debbie said. "What do you want them for anyway?"

"Why should I tell you?" Tania tilted her head. *God help me, but this mouthy brat is starting to grow on me,* she thought. *Shame she and her friend will have to be silenced.*

"They're my friends. If you're going to take them, I have a right to know."

Tania grinned. "Okay then. If you must know, I'm going to sell them to a very bad man who is going to give me a lot of money for them. And do you know what *he's* going to do with them?"

Debbie refused to respond.

"He's going to make them fight. Dogs, mostly. Big nasty, mean old dogs with huge teeth dripping with blood. Maybe he'll make them fight each other too. And when they're too old or sick - or dead - to fight anymore he's going to skin them and stuff them and mount their heads on his office wall so he can look at them every day and be reminded of all the lovely money people paid him to watch them fight."

"You can't do that! I won't let you!"

"Oh, I can and I will."

"No you won't." Debbie grinned back at Tania with a confidence that made her take a step back. "Me and Ty are going to stop you. Just wait and see."

***

Ty's ankle was aching again. The numbing effect of the cold water was wearing off. He stopped at the top of a slope and sighed. It was steep and uneven and dark but he was going to have to climb down there if he wanted to get back to his bike. Stepping carefully, he scrambled down the embankment until he felt loose rubble under his feet.

The railway.

I must be nearly back at the car park, he thought. *I can make it.*

Off in the woods, not too far away, he heard that dog bark again followed by a shout.

"That's it Reggie, you find him!"

"Oh crap," he said, eyeing up the bank he'd have to climb up again. It was too steep. He'd never make it before they got here. He squinted to see where the railway tracks went, but they seemed to wind off deeper into the woods, back towards his hunters.

There was only one way to go.

Slowly he turned around, knowing what was behind him. Something he'd deliberately avoided looking at. It had been bad enough in the daylight.

The boarded up tunnel loomed over him like a gigantic monster-mole, burrowing out of the earth, opening wide to swallow him whole. Through the darkness he could make out the piece of corrugated iron Debbie had pulled back earlier.

"I'm going to have to go in, aren't I?" he said to - well he wasn't quite sure who. Himself? God? Moritasgus? All of the above?

As he crept over the ballast he saw something in the shadow of the opening, something that hadn't been there before. What was that? He couldn't tell. It was white and seemed to glow in the moonlight. Then it moved.

Ty stopped and yelped, but didn't take his eyes off the thing. He leaned forward to get a closer look. Two small black dots peered back at him. As his eyes became accustomed to the dark he could make out the telltale stripes of a badger. No... just one stripe. One half of its face was completely white.

"Bert?" he whispered. "Is that you?"

The creature shuffled away, squeezing through a slit between the boards and vanishing into the tunnel.

With a sigh, Ty approached the gap the badger had opened. As he reached the entrance he saw that graffiti again:

BEWARE THE CONDUCTOR

As he read the last word, that faint, high pitched whistling started up again, making his skin prickle and his ears hurt.

"It's only the wind. It's only the wind," he said to himself as he squeezed into the tunnel.

WHERE'S YOUR CHILD TONIGHT?

Tim breathed a heavy sigh. He'd been looking forward to a quiet night in. No Debbie, no noise, no mess. Just him, a twelve inch pepperoni pizza from the delivery place, a four pack of Czech beers and a proper, grown up action film on the telly. Not one of those horse films that Debbie liked so much but a proper, gung ho, over-the-top gore fest with Arnie or Stallone or Van Damme or someone like that.

But the pizza had been bland, the beer had achieved nothing but to give him a pounding headache after just half a bottle and he'd continually nodded off through the film, despite all the explosions and car crashes.

He picked up the newspaper from the coffee table and scanned the front page. The main headline declared: DESIGN FAULTS TO BLAME FOR CAR PARK DISASTER and further down the page in smaller letters: MYSTERY BODY STILL UNIDENTIFIED, POLICE SAY.

Ugh, death and destruction. Just what I need to cheer me up before bed.

He pushed himself up and out of the chair, threw the paper back onto the table and, with a wide yawn, switched the light off and made his way out of the room, leaving the half-eaten pizza in its box on the sofa for any mice lucky enough to find it.

"Might as well have an early night," he muttered as he

made his way up the stairs.

Except after half an hour of staring at the ceiling he just couldn't drift off at all. With a sigh he leaned over and pressed the button on his bedside clock. Its bright red display informed him that it was half-past-ten. On a normal work night he'd be long asleep by this time and even on a Friday night he'd probably be dozing on the sofa while Debbie watched something she wasn't supposed to.

"What the hell is wrong with me?" he whispered as he climbed out from under his duvet and felt his way to down the corridor towards the bathroom, grabbing his phone from the wireless charger on the way.

As he stumbled in the darkness, he paused at Debbie's door. He lifted his hand to the wooden plaque bearing the motto:

Debbie Lives Here and You Don't!

He slowly ran his finger along the letters of her name and smiled when he remembered the look on the face of the man on the engraving stall at the fair when he asked her what she wanted it to say and if she'd like any pictures.

"A fox in a fighter plane, shooting the shit out of a huntsman!"

"Debbie! Language!"

"Er... wouldn't you like a nice unicorn or something?" the man had said, flicking through his folder of designs in a blind panic.

"No! But... Can you do a nasty unicorn?"

"I don't think I—"

Tim leaned in and whispered, "Just do your normal unicorn and tell her its name is Bloodspike The Destroyer or something, yeah?"

As his eyes adjusted to the gloom, he squinted at Bloodspike. He had been a lovely unicorn, exquisitely engraved, but Debbie had drawn little black triangles on his teeth with a marker pen so they looked like fangs, scribbled furious eyebrows above its eyes and... Was that red nail varnish dripping from its horn?

He pushed open Debbie's door gently, being careful not to wake—

Idiot. She's not even here.

He stepped inside and glanced around. For such a chaotic person, it was surprisingly tidy. All her books and DVDs were on the bookcase and her clothes were folded on her chair.

Her cuddly toys, lined up along the windowsill, caught the streetlight's glare through the open curtain and cast bizarre shadows on the floor. They looked like they were immersed in some weird, arcane ritual. He shuddered as an earworm slithered into his mind. The Teddy Bears' Picnic.

He stared into the shadows and something on her bedside cabinet caught his eye as it reflected the streetlight. He stepped further into the room and picked it up. It was a book. He held it up against the orange glow from outside.

FORGOTTEN
FOLK TALES
OF DAXONSHIRE

This had been Claire's when she was little, given to her by her grandmother. The only copy left in the whole world she'd told her. Tim wasn't sure how true that claim was, but he'd never seen another copy.

He flipped the book over, running his finger across the cover, the same cover that Claire had held so many times. She used to read from it every night for Debbie. Claire's favourite had been the one with the priest who made friends with a badger but since...

He paused, took a deep breath and closed his eyes.

Since Claire wasn't here anymore he'd read from it for Debbie instead - but not for a year or so. She was too old for it, she'd said.

Although Claire had been gone almost four years, and he'd been seeing Amanda for one of those, her absence still left a gaping chasm in his heart. He'd found ways to avoid falling down it, or to cross the divide, but whenever he was reminded of her - like now - he was hit by that same feeling, like he was falling into that deep, black hole and leaving his stomach behind.

As he fingered the binding, something brushed against his thumb. He opened his eyes. It was the tassel from a bookmark. He flipped the book open to the page that held it. It was the giraffe one that came with the wildlife conservation stationery set he'd got her for Christmas.

She was still reading it.

Without him.

There was that falling sensation again. He looked at the page to see which one she was currently on.

ELEANOR CULPEPPER
& THE CROSSROADS BOOK[1]

He laughed out loud which sounded weird in the empty house. It was that nasty fairy story about the farm girl and the mysterious gentleman on the road who gave her a book which, when she read it... He screwed up the corner of his mouth as the brutal images that he'd tried to forget drifted back into his mind's eye. Debbie, of course, had loved it because the heroine had, as she'd put it, kicked butt.

Well, she loved most of it. Even though he'd read it to her every single night for a month, she always made him skip over the part with...

He shook his head.

I hated that story but I'd give anything to be reading it to her right now.

He slid the bookmark back between the pages, closed the book and placed it back on her bedside cabinet before leaving the room.

***

As he sat on the toilet he unlocked the phone with his fingerprint. He'd intended to check his text messages but accidentally caught the Call History icon instead. The last call had been that weird one with Amanda this afternoon.

That's odd, he thought. *Debs normally calls me to say night-night when she stays with her friends.* Memories of her refusal to accept his lift came back and

---

[1] Eleanor's adventure is included as a bonus story at the back of this book.

he bowed his head. He sat there in silence for a minute or two when he decided, against his better judgement, to be the embarrassing dad.

He opened Contacts, scrolled to "Trouble" and selected Call Number. It went straight to voicemail.

"Tough luck! I'm not here, so after the beep you know what to do," came her voice, so full of attitude and fun, down the speaker. It wasn't her, not really. Not anymore.

He thought back to the question she'd asked him yesterday: *Are ghosts real?*

He was listening to one right now; the ghost of a version of Debbie who had existed a couple of years ago but was gone now. He smiled when he thought of some of the things they'd done together back then.

What's she doing now? he wondered. *Probably reading Amanda's trashy celebrity magazines or watching sitcoms she's still not old enough for.* Now he was the one going to bed early, unable to sleep until he'd heard her voice, and she was out having fun.

"Hey Debs," he said after the promised beep came. "It's your dad. Remember me? Just checking in that you're alright and having fun. I know it's past your bedtime, but I also know what you and Ty are like so if you get this any time before you *actually* go to bed, can you give your old man a ring back, okay? Talk to you soon."

He tapped the red disconnect button and stared at his phone like something was wrong with it but he just couldn't see what. Then it hit him.

It had gone to voicemail.

She wouldn't be making calls at this time of night, surely? And she was such a stickler for keeping it charged and turned on all the time. Why was her phone turned off?

Something was wrong. He wasn't sure how he could tell. He just could.

He stood back up without having used the toilet, but flushed it and washed his hands anyway. He walked back into Debbie's bedroom and flicked on the light.

After pacing around the room several times he lifted his phone and selected another number from his Contacts.

"Hey Tim," came a voice from the speaker. "How's the party at yours? Everything okay?"

"Hey 'Manda," he said. "I know it's late, and you're not well, but can I just speak to Debs for— Wait. What party?"

***

"Shanice Grant!"

"What?"

"I need a word with you, young lady!"

"I'm on the phone to Emily."

"Girl, I don't care if you're talking to Beyonce herself. Say goodbye and get your arse down here now!"

"What for?"

"Never you mind what for. If you're not down here in ten seconds then–"

"Okay! Okay! I'm coming!"

Amanda watched from the lounge as the teenager stropped down the stairs with all the attitude she would have done thirty years ago if her parents had called her down in such a manner. It would have been comical if this wasn't so serious.

Shanice leaned on the door frame and huffed.

"What?" she said, biting her bottom lip.

"Where's your brother?"

"He's staying at Mr Carter's house with Debbie."

"I'll ask you again, and you'd better tell me the truth this time. Where is your brother?"

"Mum! I already told you. He. Is. Staying. At. Mr Carter's."

Amanda kicked the door. It swung fully open revealing Tim sitting next to her on the sofa, arms crossed. The adults both looked up at her.

This time Tim spoke.

"Hello Shan. Where's my daughter?"

Realising she was cornered, she turned to Amanda. "Listen, Mum. They made me do it, okay?"

"Oh I know all about your little phone call," Amanda said. "Feeling ill, am I? You'll be the one feeling ill if you don't tell me—"

"Alright!" Shanice shouted. "Yes, I covered for them. But I don't know where they went. Ty promised me that it wasn't dangerous."

"That what wasn't dangerous?" Tim said.

"I don't know, honestly. He wouldn't tell me. All I know is that he said it was important, and that he would bring me photos back."

"Photos of what?" Amanda said.

"I. Don't. Know," Shanice snapped. "Wait. They're not in trouble are they?"

"Oh, they will be. All three of you will be once we find them."

Shanice paced back and forth in the lounge doorway, replaying the conversation with her brother from earlier in her head.

"He said it was safe."

"What was that?"

"Shush. I'm talking to myself. Let me think a minute," she glared at Amanda who backed off immediately. "It's safe, he said. I'll have my phone with me. I'll ring in the morning from... where did he say he'd ring from?"

She paced around a few more times.

"From the cottage. That's what he said. The cottage."

"Where the hell is the cottage?" said Amanda. "Which cottage?"

Tim leapt up, grabbing his car keys and phone from the table.

"I know exactly where they are. Come on."

RAILWAYS ARE
NOT PLAYGROUNDS

The tunnel was even blacker than Ty imagined it would be. The only light, once he'd done his best to push the boards and corrugated iron back into place, was from a thin shaft of moonlight streaming through a tiny gap at the top of the barrier. It didn't really help, apart from illuminating the ceiling which was thick with dark, slimy moss.

There were noises in here. Mostly the constant drip, drip, drip of the damp ceiling, but the occasional creak. There most definitely were animals in here too. He could hear them scurrying about. Rats, probably.

And of course, there was that whistle.

"Oh crap. The Conductor."

But from inside the tunnel, it sounded less like a guard's whistle, and more like, well, just the wind whipping through a big brick tube. In fact the sound wasn't coming from deeper in the tunnel, it now sounded like it was coming from outside.

"That's weird."

Curiosity got the better of him and he crept back to the boarded up entrance, leaning his head in towards one of the metal sheets he'd climbed under. Was it the metal itself that was whistling? He reached out and placed a hand on the iron. It was vibrating and sent a buzzing sensation from his fingers, up his arms and all the way down to his back. Not only that, but the whistling had stopped too. He pulled his hand away from the metal. The shrill noise started up again.

Ty hadn't realised that he had been holding his breath, and upon discovering that The Conductor was nothing more than simple physics, he let out a huge sigh of relief.

A gruff wail came from the dark. Not as high-pitched as the fox in the woods from earlier, and not as deep or threatening as a dog. A second yelp echoed around the tunnel.

"Bert? Is that you? I can't see."

He took off his backpack and rummaged around in it, pulling out a small LED torch. He flicked it on and pointed it around the tunnel. It was mostly empty, the curve of the track vanishing off into the black interior of Graveling Hill, further than his torch could penetrate, but there was something in here; a tattered old armchair whose springs looked like they had collapsed a long time ago and some old sheets.

Minding his footing on the gravel he stepped closer to the chair, keeping the torch focused on the ground beneath him. As he approached, a glistening nose and two gleaming black eyes came into view from behind it, reflecting the torchlight.

"There you are," Ty said, crouching down and pulling his syrup and bowl from the bag. He poured out a small amount, put the bowl down and stepped back.

The creature shuffled out of the darkness, snuffling its way towards the bowl. When it reached its goal it looked up at him. It was the same badger as before. Half of its face was normal, with a black stripe running from its nose all the way up to the top of its head. The other side was, aside from that tiny eye, completely white.

They looked at each other for several seconds. Ty wanted to reach out and stroke it but somehow he knew this would be wrong, so instead he looked deep into the badger's gaze. After a little while longer the animal tucked into the sweet treat in the bowl. When it had finished it looked up at Ty again, licking a drop of syrup from the end of its nose.

While they regarded each other, a clattering came from near the tunnel mouth, followed by barking and muttering. Ty and the badger both looked up at the boarded up entrance.

"Reggie, good boy! Did you find something? Seek it! Go on."

The dog was scratching and scraping at the gravel around the barricade.

When Ty looked back to the badger, it was already shuffling away, deeper into the tunnel.

"Wait for me," he said and followed it.

Just as they reached the curve in the track Bert stopped and turned to his right, seemingly vanishing into the wall. Ty shone his torch at the area where the badger had been. There was an open door leading to a small room. He followed Bert in, and quietly closed the door, just as he heard Benny pulling the board back and stepping into the tunnel.

"I know you're in here Ty."

How does he know my name?

"Reggie can smell you. Come out before I come in there."

Ty flicked on the torch again and wildly shone it around the small room, looking for another way out. It was some kind of storeroom, probably used by the old railway workers back in the olden days. In the corner was a wooden box marked with faded words that looked like they had once said:

LOST PROPERTY

He ferreted through the blankets and clothing looking for something, anything that could help him get out of this situation. As he neared the bottom of the box, his fingers connected with something long and cylindrical.

A metal bar? A baseball bat?

He pulled the object out and shone his torch at it. It was a walking stick with a carved badger head, just like Debbie's.

"What? How did this get here?" he whispered to Bert.

Footsteps crunched through the ballast outside. They were almost at the door.

"Now how did she do it?" he said, sticking his fingers into the badger's mouth. It swung open. He looked into the shaft. There was something inside. He twisted the cane and, just as with the key to Bert's house, something rose out of the middle. Ty plucked it out, closed the badger's mouth and turned the object around in his hands.

He grinned.

"Oh, yeah! I think I can use this."

***

"Debbie."

She looked up. Where was that voice coming from?

"Debbie."

There it was again.

"Hello?" she whispered.

"Behind you. It's Will."

She tried to twist around to see, but the restraints were too tight. She was still stuck.

"Oh it's you! Get away from me."

"Shhh. Tania will hear." Will crawled around towards her until he came into the corner of her vision. He held his finger up to his lips. "Listen. I never meant to hurt anyone. We didn't know there was anyone here."

"You hurt Ty!"

"I was lying. He only twisted his ankle. He was fine when I last saw him. He saved my life so I owe him one. As long as Benny doesn't find him he'll be safe."

"But you want to make the badgers fight."

Will paused. "I don't want to see them get hurt any more than you do."

"What did you think the cages were for?"

"I didn't realise. I thought we were just going to sell them as pets or something."

"Badgers aren't pets."

"Well, they're your pets aren't they?"

"They are not! They're my friends, my family, but they're most definitely not my pets."

"Okay, okay, I'm sorry. Listen," he leaned in closer, checking to see what Tania was doing. She was pacing back and forward, holding her phone up to the moon. "I'm going to cut the cable ties, okay?"

Debbie nodded.

"And then you have to get the hell out of here. Run. Get the police, your mum and dad, anyone. I'll try to stall her, yeah?"

She felt the snick of the plastic as the knife sliced through. Blood flowed back into her fingers. They prickled with pins and needles.

"I'm not leaving my friends behind."

Will crawled on his belly towards Debbie's feet, keeping one eye on Tania. He sliced through the second cable tie. More pins and needles, this time in the ends of her toes. She wiggled her feet as they came back to life.

"Anyway, she's got something of mine and I want it back."

***

Reggie was now at the door. It would be seconds before Benny got there.

"Ready?" Ty said to Bert. He liked to think that the badger nodded back at him. He pushed the door open a fraction and the room burst into life. Reggie was in, barking and whining, knocking things over, clattering into shelves and furniture.

From outside Benny heard the ruckus and scrambled over the ballast to see what was going on. Then the iron door burst open with a clang that reverberated all the way down the tunnel and Bert shot out, closely pursued by the dog.

He turned away to watch the two animals.

"Oh crap! That's the last badger. Reggie! Reggie! Get him!" he bellowed as the badger and the dog vanished through the barrier, out into the open again.

"Yo! Benny!"

He spun around to see who had called him.

***

Debbie tiptoed around the edge of the trees, never taking her eyes off of Tania, who was getting more and more worked up at the lack of phone reception. She couldn't see the gun. Tania must have put it in her pocket. She could, however, see the cane. It was jammed into the soil, just to Tania's right.

If I can just reach that then I'll have the key to Bert's house and I can call for help.

Once she'd got as close as she could without having to break her cover, Debbie crept up behind Tania. Slowly, carefully.

When she was almost there she heard furious barking off in the distance followed by a dismayed voice crying out:

"Reggie! Reggie! Get him!"

Tania turned toward the commotion.

This is my chance.

Debbie lunged forward without thinking. She froze and grimaced as she heard the crack of a twig under her feet.

Crap.

Just as Tania began to turn towards her another voice to their left cried out.

"Tania! The girl. She's gone."

She turned away from Debbie, reaching into her pocket.

"Shit! Get off your arse and find her! Now!" Tania pulled the gun out.

Thanks Will.

Debbie pulled the cane out of the ground and spun it around in her hands.

"Hey! Bitch Face!"

Tania turned around to see who had called her.

***

The kid swung the cane like a cricket bat and the solid badger-headed handle connected with the chin of the crook who went down on their back, smacking their head on the hard ground. The thunderous crack coupled with the scream of anger and pain sent previously sleeping birds fluttering nervously out of their treetop roosts.

A second blow to the stomach forced all of the air out of the crook's lungs.

A third to the side of the head and everything went grey and blurry.

The last thing the badger baiter saw before unconsciousness devoured them was the kid looming over them, holding a carved badger head at the end of their nose.

***

"And stay down!" said Ty.

***

"I told you this was mine!" said Debbie.

HARD ROAD

Once Ty had checked that Benny was out cold and not likely to get up any time soon, he quickly made his way out of that horrible, creepy tunnel, sealing the entrance up as best he could in case Benny woke up and tried to chase him. He was glad to be out of there.

That place most definitely didn't want him there. He could feel it in every shiver in his chest, in the hairs on the back of his neck - even in his teeth - that he wasn't welcome. As soon as he stepped out onto the moonlit overgrown track those feelings of dread and utter loneliness immediately flitted away, as if he'd changed TV channels from Extreme Horror Network to 24/7 Kidtoons.

Reggie was also gone, although Ty could hear the dachshund yapping through the trees, still in hot pursuit of Bert he presumed.

With Benny out of commission and the one they called Will, seemingly on his side now, he decided to go back and help Debbie and the badgers. He wouldn't be able to live with himself if he'd left her to get help and - he shuddered to even think it - something had happened to her.

Using the cane he'd found in the tunnel, he made his way back up the bank in the direction of Bert's house. Once he'd reached the top, he froze, his breath still rapid and shallow from the climb, but becoming even faster with panic when the shade from the trees left a cover of shadow so dark that he couldn't see the Grey Path back to the house.

As he stood there in the dark, not knowing what to do next, tears began to gather in the corner of his eyes. He wiped his eyes and sniffed the remainder of the tears and snot back up.

Then he heard the voice.

It was barely audible, just on the very edge of his hearing through the midnight sounds of the wood, but it was quite clearly a voice.

He glanced over his shoulder, back towards the tunnel. Nothing. The voice had come from the forest. He squinted into the trees.

There it was again. Slightly louder this time. And it was close. Very close.

He recognised the words, words that just a few hours ago he had never heard before:

"Moritasgus Ambulat."

He held his breath when he realised that he not only recognised the words but the voice. It was his own.

"Moritasgus Ambulat," he said again, this time louder. It hadn't made any sense before but now he had a strange sensation, like a tingle inside his own head; he understood. He closed his eyes, whispering the words over and over.

As he focused on the words, he felt the rapid rise and fall of his chest slow to long deep breaths. He squeezed his fists tight and focused all of his thoughts on Debbie and the caged badgers. As he concentrated, the strangest sensation flooded over him, like he was shrinking, crouching down, lower and lower, until he was as good as lying face down in the soil. And although his eyes were still scrunched tightly shut, he could see everything. The trees, the sky, the moon, the long grass and brambles, but most of all, the Grey Path back to the river. Where everything else around him was shrouded in darkness, the track seemed to glow. How had he missed it before?

Without opening his eyes, he took a step forward, then another and another until he was running. It felt like he was playing one of his VR games on his PlayStation. He picked up speed as each twist and turn of the path presented itself to him. Every gnarled tree root and hidden animal burrow, things he might easily have tripped on, were easy to see and avoid. He crossed the river with ease, just running through it and up the other side, not caring as he felt the ice cold of the water splashing around him.

Is this what Debbie meant about knowing where the land wants me to go? he thought.

Despite the throb in his ankle, he sprinted back through the wood until he was close to the sett, and trouble.

***

"Benny? Is that you?" Will said as the bushes behind the cages rustled. "Stay back there," he said, holding an arm out to keep Debbie behind him. Will bent down, picked up a spade and stepped forward, raising it above his head.

From the darkness they both heard heavy breathing. Debbie raised a hand to her throat. It still ached from when Benny had grabbed her by the back of her t-shirt earlier.

"Who's there?" Debbie yelled.

Will turned to her and held his fingers to his lips. Her eyes widened in shock and then her entire face broke into a huge grin. He tilted his head in confusion as she rushed towards and then past him.

"Ty!" she cried, thrusting her arms around him, before she leapt away in disgust. "Urgh! You're *soaking*! And filthy!"

"Yeah," he said, squeezing water out of his hoodie. "I'm glad to see you too."

Will stepped forward and ruffled his hair. "I owe you one, little man," he said.

Ty smiled and looked at the floor in embarrassment.

Will grasped him by the shoulders. "Look at me," he said.

Ty tilted his eyes towards Will's.

"I would be dead now if you'd carried on running. And I wouldn't have blamed you if you had."

Will grabbed him by the hand and pumped it up and down, then grabbed him by the back of the head and pulled him into an embrace.

Ty tried to say "It was nothing," but through Will's gilet it came out as "If nubbin."

Will released him from the bear hug.

"What happened to the woman? The leader?" Ty said.

"Tied up," Debbie said. "We called the police from the phone in Bert's house. They said they'd get here soon, but who knows when that'll be. What about the other one, Benny?"

"Well, he's knocked out in the tunnel."

"How did you manage that?" she said.

"I had a little help from–" He paused. "Wait! The badgers! We have to get these guys out." He turned to the nearest cage and tried to release the catch. As before, it was too tight to pull open. He turned back to Will. "Is there a key?"

"I had the key, but I must have dropped it when I fell in the river. The police will have something to get them out."

"No! We have to do it now. And I've got an idea."

Debbie watched as Ty pulled what appeared to be a stick out of the bush he'd crawled from. He lifted it up into the light. She gasped.

"It's a cane just like mine!" she said.

"Not quite like yours," he said, pulling the badger-head mechanism open and sliding a multi-tool out of the carved creature's mouth. He flicked one of the attachments out from under the handle.

"We can use this," he said, snipping through the cage's wires with the pliers as if it were his mum cutting through knitting yarn with scissors.

BADGER GIRL

Fourteen of the twenty-six cages had been opened by the time the car lights flickered through the trees.

They'd released the cubs first before moving onto the adults. Most of the badgers had run from their cages straight into their hole in the ground but Hattie gently nudged each of the children's shoes with her nose first. Debbie gave Will an "I'm sorry," shrug of the shoulders when Hattie turned her back on him and followed her cubs into the sett. He screwed up the corner of his mouth and raised his right eyebrow.

"I don't blame her."

All three turned to look as the car's lights, even from way over at Bert's house, lit up the clearing, sending shadows of leaves and branches playing and dancing across the grass.

"It's the police at last!" Ty said.

The slam of a car door cut through the calm of the wood.

"Debbie? Debbie?" came a man's voice, bellowing through the trees. A woman was calling Ty's name too.

"Oh no," Debbie said. "That doesn't sound like the police."

"No," Ty said. "But that does."

Far in the distance, right at the edge of her hearing she could just hear the wail of a siren. As it grew louder the forest canopy began to throb with an unnatural blue light.

The yelling voices stopped for a second. One of them, the man, shouted "What in the hell is going on?"

Debbie rubbed her forehead and temples, which were now throbbing.

"He wasn't supposed to find out," she said. "Bert didn't want him to know. He wouldn't understand."

"Who?" Will said.

"My dad, that's who! And he's going to kill me!"

"And my mum too," said Ty. "We are so dead."

***

Tim turned towards the pulsating blue glow as it grew brighter, heading towards him down the drive of Bert's house. He raised a hand to shield his eyes from the flashing. The siren ceased and through the glare he saw two figures emerge from the vehicle. As they came into view, the one who had climbed out of the passenger seat spoke.

"Tim?" she said. "Tim Carter?"

Still dazzled by the lights, Tim squinted until he could make out the woman's features.

"Cally? Is that you?"

As Sergeant Lisa Callaghan came into view she tilted her head and scratched at her temple.

"What are you doing out here Tim?" she said.

"We're looking for Debbie and her friend. What are *you* doing out here?" he said.

"We received an anonymous call about a gang of out-of-towners disturbing some of the local badger habitats. The call was made from the phone in old Bert's house," she paused. "Wait. You think Debbie's out here in the woods? Badger baiters are dangerous folks! We'd better find her, and fast."

"And my son," said Amanda. "His name is Tyrese Grant."

"Don't worry," Cally rested a hand on Amanda's shoulder. "We'll find them. Come on." She flicked on her torch and pointed it into the undergrowth. The bushes rustled and shook.

As Cally leaned in to take a closer look the bushes parted and a quiet voice, through the noise, said: "We're already here."

Debbie, Ty and Will stepped into the torchlight. All three of them held up their hands to protect their eyes. Cally flicked the torch off.

Amanda ran to her son and pulled him tight into her chest.

"Oh my God, we've been so worried. Look at you!" she said as Ty's damp clothes squelched in her hands. "You're filthy! And you're soaking wet! You'll catch your death out here in the cold and dark!"

Debbie tiptoed towards her dad, took his hand in hers and looked up to him. But he wasn't looking at her. He was looking at the man who had followed her and Ty out of the woods.

"Who are you?" he whispered.

"What was that, Dad?"

He let go of her hand and rushed towards Will, grabbing him by the collar with both hands.

"Who are you? And what are you doing out here in the middle of the night with two ten-year-old kids?" he screamed into Will's face.

Will did not attempt to defend himself, allowing Tim to thrust him up against the wall of the house, pressing so hard that he felt his feet leave the ground.

Tim shook with rage. The vein that always stood out on the side of his head whenever he was telling Debbie off looked like it was going to explode. He didn't hear or feel, or maybe was just ignoring, his daughter pounding his side with her fists.

"Let him go! Let him go! Will helped us!"

"Tim!" Amanda cried out. "Stop it!"

But Tim continued to press himself into Will, his fists clenching so hard that they turned red and then white.

"I'm going to kill you," he roared into Will's face. He continued to push until he felt a hand gently touch his shoulder and a voice whisper in his ear.

"Tim," Cally said. "Let him go. Don't make me stop you."

Tim glared into the frightened man's face and very slowly released his grasp. Will slid down the wall and collapsed into a heap on the floor.

Cally crouched down beside him.

"Will, is it?"

He nodded.

"What happened here? Can you tell me?"

Again, Will nodded. He took a moment to gather his breath back. He pointed to the Land Rover.

"In there. It was her idea. I didn't know—" His sentence was cut off as he choked back a sob.

"It's okay." Cally rested a hand on his knee. She turned to her fellow officer, Constable Finn and tilted her head towards the car. He nodded in silent agreement and walked to the car, shining his flashlight through the vehicle's windows.

"There's someone in here. A woman. Oh my God, I think she's—"

"Unconscious," Will said. "She's only unconscious."

"Will," Cally said. "Who is it? Did you do this?"

"No! I did," Debbie said, stepping forward, her left hand on her hip. "I knocked her out with this." She planted the cane into the ground.

"Why?" Cally said.

"Why? She was going to take my badgers! Then she said she was going to kill them! I think she was probably going to kill me too! That's why?"

Tim slid down the wall and slouched next to Will, his head in his hands. "You shouldn't even be out here!"

"It's lucky I was!"

"You lied to me and you lied to Amanda. Don't you realise how worried we were? Anything could have happened to you."

"Er, Sarge?" Finn called over from the Range Rover. "Sorry to interrupt and all that."

Cally nodded.

"She's going to be okay I think. She'll probably need her head seeing to. There's a nasty lump. Concussion I reckon."

"Call an ambulance, then the station. Get another squad car out here. She'll need to be restrained and accompanied at the hospital." She turned back to Will. "You know you're going to have to face the consequences too? It's up to six months in prison and a five thousand pound fine for removing or harming badgers."

He nodded without taking his head from his hands.

"Will, no," Debbie whispered. She took his hand away from his face and held it in her own.

"It's alright," he said. "I knew what I was doing was wrong. I just didn't realise how wrong." He turned to Cally. "I'll tell you whatever you want."

"Thank you." Cally smiled and patted his knee. "And I'll do everything I can to get your sentence reduced." She stood up, walked to the edge of the wood and squinted as she shone her torch through the trees at the stack of cages. "The two of you have been busy," she said.

"Huh?"

"There must be twenty or more cages and you've made a right mess of the forest floor here. That's a lot of work for two people in one night."

"Three. There were three of us."

Cally turned back toward the group.

"Three? Where is–"

"He's in the old railway tunnel." Ty wrestled himself from his mother's grasp and stood beside Debbie.

"And how do you–"

"Because I knocked him out with mine!" He thrust his own stick into the ground beside Debbie's.

"Tyrese!" said Amanda. "You didn't?"

"I did!" he said. "He was chasing me and I hid but he found me and I thought he was going to get me but Bert–"

"Bert?" said Tim.

"He's a badger. Keep up."

Tim raised his eyebrows.

"So Bert distracted him and while his back was turned I was like "Yo Benny!" and he was all like "What?" and I was like "Eat this!" and I smacked him in the face."

Cally crouched down so she was the same level as the two ten-year-olds.

"You know what you did here tonight was incredibly dangerous and stupid?"

"But—"

She placed her finger on Debbie's lips.

"But," she paused to make sure there would be no further interruptions. "It was also very, very brave. Should you have run away and called us right away? I'd say yes. Might that have resulted in them getting away with it? Possibly. We can't really play 'What If', but it is clear that despite the lying and the violence - which I cannot condone - that these creatures," she pointed back at the cages, "would be in serious trouble if not for the pair of you. You saved their lives."

"And mine."

Everyone whipped their heads towards Will.

"Yeah. He saved me from drowning. I owe him big time."

"Oh, Ty," Amanda sniffed back tears.

Tim climbed up from the floor, walked over to Debbie and put his arms around her neck.

"You should have told me what you were doing tonight. I might have come with you, you know?"

This time it was Debbie sniffing back tears. She nodded.

"I'm sorry Dad. I wanted to look after the badgers."

"You did! I'm proud of you. Bert would have been proud of you too."

"Does that mean you won't punish me?" She wiped her nose with her sleeve and gave him an innocent smile.

"Absolutely not!"

"Aaaah, Dad! That's so not fair!" She paused. "Actually, there's one other thing I probably should tell everyone."

"What's that?" Cally said.

"I took this off the woman, Tania. You'll probably want it."

She slipped her backpack from her shoulders and rummaged around. She produced a silver-coloured object and held it up so that the moonlight glinted off it.

"Jesus Christ," said Finn. "She's got a shooter!"

***

"Ty?"

Debbie leaned over and whispered in his ear and poked his side as the car trundled along the potholed country road away from Penlock Forest.

"Are you awake?"

"I am now." He rubbed the crust of sleep, and a fair amount of mud and dirt from the corner of his eyes. He looked at his soiled fingers and rubbed them on his hoodie. It was ruined anyway.

"I had the weirdest dream just now," she said.

"Oh yeah? What happened?"

"I was walking through the woods, and it was dark, like tonight, but the next thing I knew I was a badger snuffling and running around on the forest floor. And even though it was dark, I could easily see where I was going. Anyway, I ran and ran until I got to the Walburg Sycamore where I stopped and turned back into me."

"That's weird." Ty cocked his head.

"Yeah. Anyway, I was stood there looking at the tree and I could see that there was someone hiding behind the tree and I said "Who's there?" but they just stayed there. Then it got all quiet and all I could hear was a voice whispering those words from Bert's Wi-Fi, remember? Moritasgus Ambulat?"

Ty nodded. He was now wide awake, keen to hear the rest of the dream.

"Then the person in the shadows stepped out into the light and - get this - it was also me! And the other me stood in front of me and said it again in my face and I was like 'What do you mean?' and she said 'We are Moritasgus,' so I said 'Who me, or someone else?' and she said 'Yes,' and I was all confused so I went in the house and I washed my face in the bathroom. Anyway, when I looked in the mirror guess what?"

"What?" Ty said.

"It was you!"

"Me?"

"Yeah! You were me and I was you! So we held hands and went back out and we both shrunk down into badgers and went into the sett entrance and that was when I woke up."

Ty's mouth hung open. "The same thing happened to me!"

"What? You just had the same dream?"

"No! I mean when I was in the woods on my own I felt like I was close to the ground and I could see in the dark and I thought I could hear the words."

"Woah! What do you think it means?" Debbie said, followed by a huge yawn.

"What are you two up to back there," Tim said from the driver's seat. "I'd have thought you'd be out like a light by now."

"Nothing Dad, just had a weird dream, that's all."

"Well try to get some sleep, alright. It's way past your bedtime and it'll be twenty minutes before we get home."

"Okay Dad," she said.

"Same goes for you young man," said Amanda. "Get some rest now. You and your sister will need the energy for all the chores I've got planned for you over the weekend."

"Aaah, Mum!"

In the foot well Ty's bag shook and lurched. He took the remains of his supper from the side pocket and unfastened the cord of the main compartment. A small black nose poked out of the bag and sniffed at the cheese sandwich.

"Shhh Reggie, there's a good boy," he whispered, slipping the dachshund a morsel. Reggie's tongue shot out and tugged the piece of sandwich from his hands. It was gone in two bites.

Debbie giggled quietly as she stroked Reggie's head. The dog basked in the attention and snacks.

"Maybe leave it a bit longer before you tell your Mum about him, yeah?"

EPILOGUE:
THE FINISHING LINE

Benny had to check that his eyes had actually opened at first because all he could see, aside from the white flashes of light that accompanied each twinge of pain in his throbbing head, was blackness.

He shook his head and groaned. Everything ached, especially his chin. He rubbed it but quickly pulled his hand away at the searing pain, bringing tears to his eyes.

That damn kid got me good and proper.

The ground beneath him was hard and uneven, the large chunks of rubble poking into his back and shoulders.

And it was cold. So cold.

He shivered, rubbing his arms to warm them up.

He pushed himself up onto his elbows with a grunt.

That's better he thought as he raised his head and a dim glow came into view.

"Reggie? Reggie?" he cried, but the only reply he got was the echo of his own voice, traversing the tracks into the underworld of Graveling Hill until it faded into silence.

He listened closely, for the tell-tale pitter-patter of his companion's tiny paws but all he could hear was a constant drip, drip, drip of the moss covered ceiling.

He reached for the torch in his pocket but pulled his hand back with a yelp when the broken glass from the now useless flashlight sliced into his thumb.

He sucked at the end of his bleeding digit, muttering "I'll get that bloody kid. When I get out of here I'm gonna find him, and I'm gonna..."

Crunch.

He stopped talking and let his injured hand fall to his side.

What was that?

Crunch.

Footsteps.

"Hello?" he whispered.

Crunch. Crunch. Crunch.

"Who's there? Reggie, is that you?"

With a click, a bright yellow light radiated from the dark, straight into Benny's face. He held up his bloodsoaked hand to protect his eyes from the dazzling aura.

"Labhesh Bendra?" came a deep voice from behind the blinding glow of the lamp.

"Who's asking?"

He squeezed his eyes through the glare. He could just make out the silhouette of a person, and just a few of their features. It was a tall man with a moustache. He was wearing a peaked hat. The light from the lamp danced like hungry flames on the surface of the chrome buttons lining his jacket.

A uniform.

Crap. It's the coppers.

"Are you Labhesh Bendra?" came the voice again, reverberating from every surface, making Benny's temples throb and his ears ring.

"What if I am?" he said followed by a cry from the

back of his throat that sounded like "Hurk!" as the man reached down, clenched his fist tightly around Benny's collar, lifted him off his behind and began to pull him deeper into the tunnel by the scruff of his neck.

Benny thrashed and clutched at the iron fist tugging him backwards into the dark, kicking and flailing at the floor, trying to get a footing sturdy enough to stand and fight back, but the ballast was loose and just too slippery for him to get to his feet.

"What do you want?"

"You really are from the wrong side of the tracks, aren't you?" said the man. "Well you've earned yourself a one-way ticket to–"

"What are you talking about? Who–"

The man pulled tighter at Benny's collar, cutting off both his breath and his words. Through the red shroud creeping across his field of vision, Benny strained to peer back at the tunnel entrance. It was a long way away now. He reached out to the tiny sliver of moonlight struggling to filter through the gap in the boards. It was fading further into blackness with every terrible crunch of the gravel.

"I'm afraid it's the end of the line for you, Benny. Didn't your parents ever teach you that railways are not playgrounds?"

***

Once the ambulance and the second patrol car had taken Tania and Will away, Cally and Finn turned to the task of freeing the rest of the badgers and collecting evidence.

She reversed the Land Rover out of the drive ready for the impound truck to collect it in the morning while Finn snipped the last of the cages open. Once all of the badgers had been returned to their home he bundled as much of the badger baiters' equipment as he could into the back of the patrol car. He stacked the remainder of the gear in the garage, locking it with the key that Tim had lent him.

"Can I ask you something Constable?" Cally asked as she walked back down the driveway towards him.

"Fire away."

"Have you been watching a lot of old cop shows recently?"

"Sarge?"

"She's got a shooter! I believe that's what you said." She laughed.

"I might have." Finn pretended to scratch an itch to hide the redness he could feel blossoming across his cheeks.

"A word of advice," she said. "Switch off from work. Watch, oh, I don't know, some science fiction on your downtime, like Constable Adhikari. You could learn a lot from her."

"Zainab's a geek? Huh? Who knew?" He shut the garage door and locked it. "We should go and look for the third one, yeah? He can't have got too–" He paused and turned towards the forest. "Did you hear that?" His entire body shuddered and he rubbed the back of his neck.

"Do you hear that?"

"Yeah," said Cally. She tipped her head into the air.

She listened for a few seconds and closed her eyes. "It's just the wind," she said eventually.

"It's giving me the creeps. Sounds more like a scream."

"It's just the wind."

"Or an old whistle, like we - coppers I mean - used back in—"

"It's just the wind, Constable." Cally turned back towards the car.

"Ma'am?"

"We'd be better off getting this stuff back to the station. I'll make sure a description gets circulated but something tells me that we won't be seeing Mr Bendra again. You ready for a long night of paperwork?"

Finn sighed and nodded. *Paperwork. They don't show that side of the job on Dempsey & Makepeace.*

Cally opened the passenger door for him. "Shall we?"

"Yeah," he said, climbing into the passenger seat and fastening his seatbelt rather more quickly than he usually would. "I think that's a very good idea. Let's get away from here."

***

As the police car receded down the lane from Debbie's house, its passengers were unaware that they were being watched. The hidden observer looked on from the shadow of the Walburg Sycamore. Once the red glow of the rear lights had faded into the night he turned and made his way towards the nearest Grey Path.

Bert smiled as he stepped between the trees and vanished back into the woods.

'Beware The Conductor' by Christopher Fieldhouse

ELEANOR CULPEPPER

& The Crossroads Book

from
*Forgotten Folk Tales
of Daxonshire*

Once upon a time, there was a young woman called Eleanor Culpepper. She lived with her father Henry on his farm between Keynford and Badgers Crossing.

There were two things Eleanor loved doing more than anything: reading and helping on the farm. During the school holidays and on weekends she worked as hard as any of the farmhands. She was almost always there before anyone else in the morning and the last to leave at night. She knew each and every new animal by name and insisted on being present at every birth to name the newborns.

As much as he appreciated her help and enthusiasm, Henry worried for Eleanor's future. He didn't like to think of her throwing her life away on an endeavour quite as unreliable as farming. He feared she'd get caught up in the same struggles he and his dear departed wife Catherine had encountered over the years.

So, as he had promised Catherine before she succumbed to the strain of Eleanor's difficult birth, he vowed that their daughter would receive the very best education that he could provide.

She could already read and write by the time she was of school age, and Henry continued to instruct her in many disciplines such as mathematics, science, literature and nature alongside her traditional school education. His hope was that one day, when she was ready, she might leave the hard life of a farmer and make something of herself in the town.

But Eleanor did not leave. She worked the farm by day and would spend her nights reading book after book, or up to her elbows in parts and grease, fixing - and even inventing - machinery to increase and improve the farm's output.

Her schoolmaster Mr Bythewood didn't know what to do with her. She often disrupted class by correcting him or asking questions he was not equipped to answer. Although he had vowed never to use the cane on a female student, what with them being far too delicate for such punishment, he often had no choice but to give her four strokes across the palm. That she didn't ever cry out in pain only enraged him further, although never quite as much as when, after lessons, he consulted the school volumes to find that she had been correct all along.

***

"Father?" she said one night as they ate at the table. "Why do they call them Accomplishments?" Seeing the look of confusion on his face, she explained. "Sometimes the boys are taken out of class and instructed in what they call Practicalities - woodwork, economics, chemistry and the like. During this time the girls are taught Accomplishments: languages, the arts, housekeeping and so on. Surely those things the boys learn are also accomplishments. Only today I asked: 'Is it not an accomplishment to turn a breached lamb, or to harness a horse for tilling?' and–"

"What did Bythewood make of that?"

She said nothing, only turned over her left hand. Fading red stripes patterned her palm where the bamboo had landed.

"Oh, Ellie," groaned Henry. "Why do you insist upon being so—"

"Clever? Is that what you were going to say?"

Henry shook his head. "Stubborn."

"That's not all, Father." She turned over the right hand to reveal a symmetrical markings to those on the left.

"And what were those ones for?"

"Well, one of the other students asked a question. It was a fairly simple one so when Mr Bythewood hesitated, I answered it in his stead. He said that a person of my standing should not presume to be an educator."

"And what did you say?" he said with a sigh, having a good idea of exactly what it was she'd said.

"I said that someone in the room needed to be didactic. He just looked at me, with a mix of confusion and utter contempt in his eyes, so I added homiletic, exhortative, pedagogic, disquisitional and erudite. He continued to stare at me so I said, 'An educator,' and he said that he was fully aware of what it means.

"I shouldn't have, but he was being so rude so I added 'Of what what means?' and he replied 'That word you used.'

"I asked him which word he meant and that was when the cane came out. He never answered my question."

"Oh, Ellie." Henry sighed. "Your predilection to prove yourself is going to get you into trouble one day."

"I don't like bullies, Father," she said, and winced, clenching her fist.

"I'll wet a cloth and fetch the carbolic soap," Henry said as he rose from his chair.

"Where would I be without you, Father?" she said with a smile.

She didn't hear him whisper "Far away from here, and significantly better off."

***

"Do you never think of leaving all this, Ellie?" he said to her the next night as they relaxed after supper.

She looked up from her papers and laughed. "Oh Father, you are silly. What good is all this knowledge if I can't use it to help those I care about the most." She nodded towards Henry and his sheepdog Bess, who slept before the fire.

"I just worry for you," he said. "That's all. How will you find a husband when you spend every hour either on the farm or buried in a book?"

"Father, really," she said. "After school I have barely enough time to milk the cows and gather the eggs. When would I find the time to go courting? I'm perfectly happy right where I am."

"You won't be in school for much longer. What will

you do then?"

"Well, you'll just have to find more responsibilities for me on the farm, won't you?" She kissed him on the head as she passed on her way to bed, book clasped firmly under her arm. "It is a big day tomorrow, with the harvest and I'll need all the sleep I can get. I'll see you bright and early."

"Yes," said Henry as the seed of a plan began to germinate in his mind. "I'll see you when the cock crows."

***

The harvest was good and bountiful, with plenty of grain, milk, fruit and vegetables to treat the farmhands to a huge feast to thank them for their hard work afterwards.

As they ate, Henry turned to Eleanor. "Well, my dear, we've had another good year, and it's largely down to you."

"Oh Father, but..."

Henry raised a hand. "Never mind 'Oh Father this and oh Father that', I have something important to ask you."

Eleanor nodded at him to continue.

"As you've made up your mind to stay and help me when you finish school, I have considered you request for more responsibility on the farm. So tomorrow morning, I'd like you to take the best of the harvest to the Dock Market on the River Swain in town, and I'd like you to negotiate prices with the traders as they come and go on their boats taking them to and from Gilworth and beyond."

"But Father, that's always been your job."

"Aye, it has. But if you really do want to be a farmer, then you need to learn these things."

Eleanor threw her arms around him and kissed him on his cheek. "I promise I won't let you down."

Henry smiled. He already knew she would do a good job. She always did. He also knew that the market on the river would be bustling with all kinds of young, attractive and educated people from all over the county, and, although it might break it, in his heart he hoped Eleanor would meet her future husband there and finally be persuaded to leave this difficult life.

***

The next morning after the farmhands had loaded up the cart with the season's best produce, Eleanor harnessed her horse Richard to the carriage and made her way towards Badgers Crossing, with Bess sitting beside her. She waved "Hello" to the people she passed on the road and they waved back with a smile.

As the village buildings thinned out and the cart entered the open countryside her smile dropped a little as she walked through the conversation with her father two nights ago over and over in her mind.

He clearly wanted rid of her. It was the only logical explanation. He didn't really trust her to do business at the Dock Market. She was being sent into town to meet a gentleman who would take her off his hands and make her his prize - no, conquest - to be paraded before his fellow patricians.

Lost in her thoughts, Eleanor sniffed back a tear, but she was brought back to the real world with a bump - literally. Richard threw back his head with a thunderous cry and the cart began to rock and jounce. She lifted her head. All she could see ahead, through a thick veil of mist, was a narrow dirt track.

"What happened to the road?" she whispered, patting the agitated creature, calming him. She gently urged Richard to carry on and although he obeyed, he was not happy, not one bit. He puffed and panted jets of vapour from his great nostrils and his wide, fear-filled eyes darted back and forth.

Beside her, Bess began to shake gently and give of a quiet rumble.

"What is wrong with you two?" Eleanor said, tussling the hair on Bess's head and neck. She pulled her hand away. Bess's muscles were taut.

"It's alright, girl," she said, stroking and scratching gently between the dog's ears. At the calming hand, Bess's growling subsided.

The fog began to clear and up ahead and Eleanor could just distinguish several elongated shapes, as big as a man, scattered amongst long grass and ugly looking weeds. The meadow looked as though it had been strewn with boulders the shape of coffins, arranged roughly in a circular formation. The grass inside the wreath looked pale and dead.

Another dirt path crossed their own up ahead, right through the centre of the circle.

"This must be the right way," she said, shaking the reins. Richard seemed to be on the verge of balking, but to Eleanor's surprise, he remained vigilant and trotted on towards the crossroads. "The roads around here are not much to talk of."

Richard whinnied as if in agreement.

Glad to be on their way again, she turned her thoughts back to her predicament. "Oh, Bess," she said. "What will I do? Father needs my help far more than I need a husband. I wish there was a way to..."

Before she could finish her sentence, Richard reared up on his hind legs with a shriek and Bess began to snarl, her teeth bared and her hackles raised even higher than the time an adder had found its way into the barn.

"Whoa there!" A man wearing a black suit, like those worn by the gentlemen from London that Eleanor had read about in the newspaper, stood in the road. He patted Richard's neck.

"Easy now."

The horse backed away and pawed at the dirt.

"Oh, sir! I do beg your pardon. I had got so lost in my own troubles that I didn't see you there in the road."

Richard snorted at the man nervously. Bess's lips drew back further.

Eleanor stepped down from the carriage, giving Bess a good ticking off as she did so. "Stop that, right now do you hear?" she said in the sheepdog's ear.

"It's quite alright," said the man, who dusted himself down and straightened up to greet her, smiling as she approached.

Eleanor paused as though caught in his deep, dark - almost black - eyes. Despite her wariness of strangers, especially men, she found herself smiling back.

"I really should watch where I'm going, especially at a crossroads. My dear," he said, holding out a hand. "What bothered you so that you took your eyes from the road?"

Eleanor's cheeks flushed a deep pink as she shook his hand.

"I... well... I..."

"Let me guess," said the man. "You are on your way to market... And you are desperate to impress someone..." he rubbed his chin. "Your... father?"

"Yes! How did you know?"

"Oh, I just have a... scent for these things." He tapped the tip of his nose three times and chuckled. "But why so sad? The old man has entrusted you with an important job. This is a big day."

"Well, yes, sir. But it's just that... He's making decisions for me when I already know my mind."

"I can see that you do!"

"I feel like he's writing my own story for me."

The man's dark eyes flashed with excitement. "Oh, you like stories? I'll tell you what." He picked up a black rectangular box from his side, set it down on the carriage seat, clicked two latches open on the front and lifted the lid. He rummaged around inside and pulled out a book. "It's not much but please, take this. It might cheer you up."

"What is it?" she said.

"Oh, just something that might help one..." he thought about how to end the sentence for a while. "Escape? Yes. Escape! It really is quite, quite magical."

"Oh, I couldn't possibly, sir. Not after almost running

you down. At least let me trade with you for it. Something from the cart, perhaps."

The man grinned the widest grin Eleanor had ever seen. He was pleased, that much was certain to her, but there was no joy in his eyes. They seemed to be filled with something more like longing... voraciousness... desire.

"It's very kind of you but that won't be necessary," he said. "There's only one thing I want from you."

I'm sure there is. She thought. *Father warned me about men like this.*

"And what would that be?" she said tentatively as she tried to draw out and interpret his intentions.

"Your name. That's all."

Eleanor blushed again. "Oh, do pardon my manners, sir. My name is..."

"Ah, ah, ah," he wagged his finger, then pulled a sheet of paper from his case along with what looked like a pen, but not any sort she recognised. He pressed at the end with his thumb and a small round nib, already laden with ink appeared. "Why don't you write it down for me." He pointed to the paper. "Just here at the bottom of the page. So I don't forget it later, you see."

Eleanor took the paper and she studied it closely. What at first seemed to be thin black lines appeared to be rows of print so tiny she could barely make that there were words at all. She squinted and pulled the paper close to her face.

The man snatched it away, saying "Oh, don't you worry about that old claptrap. This is just the first spare slip of paper I found at the bottom of my case."

"Are you sure? Because it looked important."

"Perfectly. It's just a leftover from an old business dealing of mine, now sadly forfeited." He held the pen out to her. "Unless..." his smile drooped to a frown. "Oh, how very insensitive of me! Forgive me. You can't write! That's it, isn't it? I just assumed that a lady of your apparent wit would be able..."

Eleanor clenched her fists and gritted her teeth.

"I am perfectly capable of writing anything I like, sir."

"Of course you are. Do forgive me." The man placed the paper down on the cart bench. Bess nipped at his fingers, but he pulled his hand back just in time.

"Bess! Stop that this instant," Eleanor said.

The dog slunk back, head bowed, knowing she was in trouble but not quite sure what for.

The man handed her the pen, pressing the end as he did, making the nib retract into its housing with a clicking sound. She took it from him and turned it over in her hands, gazing at it in wonder. It was entirely coated in gold and an intricately engraved snake with two emerald eyes the size of tiny pinheads spiralled three times around it from top to bottom. It was the most exotic thing she had ever seen that wasn't in a book.

Eleanor pressed on the snake's head with her thumb, just as the man had. The nib leapt out. She laughed with delight as she pressed the button again time and it vanished once more.

"Ahem." The man coughed into his fist. "You were saying something about being perfectly capable?" He made a gesture as though he was writing in the air.

Eleanor ceased her giggling and gave him a cold stare. Without taking her eyes off him she thrust her thumb into the snake's head. Once the nib had sprung back, she turned her eyes to the paper on the bench before her and scratched at it with the wondrous pen, imagining herself using it to carve her name into the forehead of Mr Bythewood.

"There!" She held the paper and pen out to the man defiantly.

He took them and smiled as he studied what she'd written.

"Eleanor. Eleanor Culpepper." He turned the name over on his tongue, exaggerating the Ls and the Ps. "How lovely. You have a very elegant hand, Eleanor. Your writing isn't bad either."

He laughed as he rolled back his sleeve to reveal a wristwatch unlike anything Eleanor had ever seen. The black face seemed to merge into the strap with no discernible join and there were no hands. Instead a small grey window displayed odd looking, angular numbers which changed as Eleanor watched in amazement.

"But look at the time!" He thumbed a silver dial on the side of the watch face and it chirped like a sparrow. "I mustn't keep you from your very important day. I hope you make a killing - if you'll excuse the expression - at the market. Impress your dear old dad!" He rolled his sleeve back down, covering the peculiar device.

"Oh, it's that way, if you were wondering." He jabbed his thumb in the direction they'd already been travelling. "About two more miles." He folded the paper and slipped it into his inner jacket pocket, then snapped his case shut and placed it at his side. He held his hand out to help Eleanor step up into the cart.

"And this." He placed the book on the bench beside her and patted it, making sure to stay well clear of Bess's reach. "Belongs to you now."

"Sir. I fear that I misjudged you. Forgive my effrontery. May I offer you a ride into town?" she said, shifting her weight in her seat until she was comfortable.

"Oh, no, no, no," he said, dismissing the idea with his hand as if swatting a bothersome fly away from his face. "It's very kind of you but I've been waiting a long time, and I have a feeling my ride out of here will be along quite, quite soon."

"Well, if you're sure, sir, then I'll be on my way." She gently flicked at the reigns and with a blast of his wide nostrils, Richard slowly set off. "Good day to you. Perhaps we will meet again," she called back.

"Oh, we will," he whispered. "We will." And then, much louder so she would hear over the muffled clip-clop of the hooves and the rumble of the wheels on the dirt. "I'm sure we'll be seeing each other again real soon."

"Oh, sir, wait. You didn't tell me *your*—" Eleanor turned to catch the gentleman's eye but he was gone. There was nothing but the dusty crossroads, a circle of fallen stones and a swirl of mist that danced back and forth on the breeze.

"Come on then you two," she said to the animals who both seemed far less harrowed, almost as though they'd forgotten their fears. "It's not much further to the Dock

Market."

***

"Well, how was it?" said Henry when Eleanor came through the door that night.

"It was wonderful, Father. I met so many people, and they were all either lovely or professional, or both, and..." she took a bag from her shoulder and emptied a mountain of banknotes and contracts onto the table. "We sold everything. Not a single grain of wheat left. And I took plenty of orders for next season too."

"Well, that's wonderful," said Henry, rubbing her shoulder. "I knew you could do it. But shall we save the business talk for the morning. Why don't you tell me more about these people you met. Was there anyone special?"

"Special?"

"Unusual, different. Anyone you found yourself drawn to."

"Well, there was one man..."

Henry rubbed his hands. "A man? Tell me more. How did you meet?"

"I met him on the road through the middle of a meadow, by a crossroads surrounded by large stones. He was waiting there for a carriage."

Henry scratched his head. "I don't think I know where you mean. Did you take a different road to the one I said?"

"Well," Eleanor blushed. "I admit to daydreaming on the way and getting a little lost. But the man helped me find the correct way. That was after Richard and I almost ran him over."

Henry closed his eyes and gently shook his head. "Oh, he was unharmed. I didn't actually get him."

"That's a good start. Was he handsome?"

Eleanor rubbed her chin. She could remember the unusual pen and wristwatch quite clearly but she was unable to bring the image of his face into her mind's eye. She couldn't recall whether he had actually been handsome at all, or if it was his charisma that she'd found alluring. "I suppose he was, yes," she said. "He was most definitely an intriguing gentleman, I'll say that."

Henry clapped his hands together. "Wonderful. And his name?"

"Oh! It never even occurred to me to ask until after we'd parted!"

"You never...?"

"But he took my name. I wrote it down for him. There can't be too many Eleanor Culpeppers around here, can there?"

"And what was he like?"

Eleanor thought about this for a moment, and settled on "Sophisticated. And well read."

"Sounds like a perfect match! You know I'm so very proud of you, don't you?" he said. "Come, have a drink with me while we celebrate today's successes."

Eleanor yawned. "If it's all the same, it's been a long day and I'm rather tired, and I think I'd just like to go to bed with a book." She kissed his forehead. "Goodnight Father."

"Goodnight, Ellie," said Henry. "Sleep well."

***

Once Eleanor had washed and dressed for bed, lit the lamp on her nightstand, and climbed under the blanket, she settled down to read. The book was not at all what she expected, and certainly not as special or magical as the man seemed to believe it was. As she scanned the contents page, she was disappointed to learn that it was just a collection of old children's stories, many of which she already knew and had grown out of years ago.

The first story however, which was called *The Wayward Fox* was not familiar to her, so she thought it discourteous not to try at least so she began to read.

Once upon a time, there was a mischievous little boy and his name was Andromalius.

"Andromalius? What a curious name," she whispered before reading on in silence.

After just a few minutes she put the book down with a sigh.

"At least you will look good on the bookshelf," she said through a yawn and snuffed the wick of her lamp.

***

The cockerel woke her the next morning and once she'd dressed, she came down to the kitchen to make breakfast for herself and her father. However, the kettle was already filled and sitting on the stove, still warm.

Beyond the kettle, out of the kitchen window, she saw him in the far field, running back and forward, chasing cows here and there.

Although she knew he would be annoyed, she couldn't help but laugh, the sight of him being evaded every time he got near one of the beasts was so comical. Eventually, she put on her boots and ran into the field to help him round up the animals.

"What happened?" she said as they herded the last of the cows back into the barn.

"I woke up early and couldn't get back to sleep so I came down this morning to make a pot of tea, and as waited for the kettle to boil, I opened the shutters. There were cows everywhere. In the meadow, the crops. One even got into the yard and ate my roses."

Eleanor stifled a laugh. "I'm sorry. I know you're proud of your flowers. So a broken lock then? Need me to fix it?"

"That's the strange thing. The lock is perfectly intact, but it sat atop the gatepost unfastened. I know I closed and locked it last night because I asked Jack to go back and check. It must have been some little rapscallion from the village up to no good. If I ever get my hands on them, I'll…"

"You'll ruffle their hair, give them a penny for aniseed balls and send them on their way. You're a big softy."

Henry nodded. "You've got the measure of me," he said.

"I do, and I hope you never change."

He took her by the hand and led her back to the house. "Now, about that tea. It must have gone cold by now. How about making your old man a fresh one?"

***

That night she stared at the book on the shelf as she prepared for bed.

"Perhaps I was too harsh," she whispered. "I was tired after all. I should give you another try." She plucked it from the shelf and settled down in bed to read.

Once upon a time, there was a cunning little fox and his name was Andromalius.

She stared at the page. "A fox? But yesterday it was a boy. I swear it was. I must have been even more tired than I realised," she said with a chuckle, As she read, she slowly drifted away into the embrace of sleep before being rudely awoken just a few minutes later by the book falling onto her face.

Rubbing her nose where the book had hit, she closed it, placed it on her nightstand and snuffed out the lamp.

***

"Ellie! Ellie! Wake up!" Her father hammered on her door.

Eleanor groaned. It was still dark. What was going on?

"It's the hens, quick."

She leapt out of bed and threw on some boots under

her nightgown, not bothering to put on any other clothing and ran downstairs to the henhouse, grabbing a lamp on the way.

She ducked down under the threshold and clambered into the henhouse, putting the lamp down as she crawled on her hands and knees through the hay and something... wet?

She looked at her hand in confusion. A dark liquid slowly ran down her palm and onto her wrist before falling lazily to the floor in fat droplets. She raised the lamp and looked into the enclosure.

The flickering wick revealed the mutilated remains and crimson-stained feathers of the chickens littering the hay-strewn floor. Blood oozed down the walls in congealing clumps and pooled into sticky, deep, wine-red puddles. Eleanor gasped. Unconcerned by the ichor soaking into his nightclothes, Henry knelt in the mess and cradled the limp, headless body of his favourite chicken Molly in his arms.

"A fox," he spat. "After all our hard work, this is how the Lord repays me? With a bloody fox to take my hens?"

Eleanor laid her hand on his shoulder.

He rested his cheek on it. "What are we going to do, Ellie? What are we going to do?"

"Let's get some sleep. There's nothing more we can do tonight. But in the morning, let's gather the farmhands. We're going to hunt the creature and catch it. And when we do I'm going to kill it."

***

As if it understood what had happened to its kin, the

cock didn't crow as dawn broke. Eleanor awoke all the same. Sleep had been difficult, interrupted by unusual dreams of chickens, and foxes, and cows and... She grimaced as she struggled to summon the details. Chickens, and foxes, and cows, and derelict stones arranged like a wreath of caskets in a mist shrouded meadow.

And the continual clicking sound of a queer, snake shaped pen.

Click. Click. Click.

As wakefulness slothfully clawed its way back, along with the realisation that the clicks were nothing more than the ticking of the Grandmother clock in the hallway.

***

Once the hands were gathered, everyone was tasked with finding and killing the fox. The cows went unmilked, the pigs unfed, the water troughs unfilled but a day's searching revealed no trace of the creature; no tracks, no scat, no new burrows in the hedgerow, and no more kills.

Exhausted and exasperated, Eleanor and her father returned to the farmhouse, too tired to do anything but fall straight into bed.

"Tomorrow, Father," she said as she kissed him goodnight at the top of the stairs. "It's a small consolation, and it won't bring the chickens back, but it's only a fox. What more harm can it do now?"

Henry just grunted, nodded and shuffled to his bedroom. The light through the slit under his door went out before Eleanor had even crossed the hallway to her own room.

She'd intended to go straight to sleep herself, but her mind was still racing with thoughts and ideas and possibilities. So she dropped the book onto her bed, ready to pick up where she left off the night before, once she'd dressed for bed. It fluttered open to the first page of the first story.

She picked it up to flick to the page she'd marked, but before she could, the first line of the story caught her eye.

**Once upon a time, there was
a creature - half man, half beast -
and his name was Andromalius.**

The book dropped from her hands and skittered along the floor until it disappeared under the bed.

"Let the damned thing stay there," she said climbing into bed. "I wish I'd never set eyes on it."

***

The next day, Eleanor was awoken by a loud bang and an ear-piercing yelp. She rushed downstairs without dressing, fearing something terrible, yet the sight before her was worse than anything she could have imagined.

Henry stood over the prone, bloodied body of Bess, rifle still pointed at the poor creature.

"Father!" she shrieked. "What have you done?"

Henry said nothing, but let the gun clatter to the floor. He sat at the kitchen table and wept into his open hands.

"Oh, my dear sweet Bess," Eleanor whispered, descending to her knees. Tears filled her eyes as she ran her hands through the blood-matted fur. She held Bess in her arms, stroking her head, whispering "It's alright Bess. I'm here. I'm here," over and over until she could no longer feel the dog's shallow breaths on her neck.

Once the initial shock had passed, Eleanor turned to Henry, her eyes filled with confusion and rage.

"Why Father? Why have you done this?"

Still overcome with emotion and unable to speak, he just pointed over his shoulder.

She followed his finger to the window, afraid to look at what lay beyond.

But look she did.

If the henhouse had been an ungodly atrocity then what greeted her eyes as she peered through the glass was an infernal vision from the very depths of Hell itself.

The meadow beyond the yard, where the sheep usually grazed, was a carpet of red. Entrails and ragged pelts of crimson-stained fleece befouled every corner of the meadow. Dead staring eyes, protruding from skinless faces gawked lifelessly, pleading - too late - for Eleanor to do something, and bloated, bloodied tongues lolled from wide-open jaws, forever petrified in screams of terror.

She clasped a hand to her mouth.

"All of them?" she said.

"No. There are three left. There were five, for a few minutes, but I had to put two of them out of their misery."

Eleanor spun on her father. "As you did with poor Bess?" she spat.

He bowed his head. "I had to."

"Why?" she screamed.

"It was never a fox. Use your eyes, girl!" Henry pointed to Bess's muzzle.

Eleanor leaned in, realising that the blood around the dog's mouth and jowls was darker and drier than that oozing from her recently ruptured flank.

"You can't think…"

"I wish I didn't but the proof is right there. It was her all along. Once she'd got a taste for blood—"

"You're wrong. Bess would never—" A sob halted the rest of the sentence and she stormed out of the room, leaving her father weeping at the table.

She thudded up the stairs, kicked the bedroom door open and clambered to her hands and knees, reaching wildly under the bed for the book. Eventually, she hooked a fingernail into the cloth cover and dragged it towards her, careful not to flick it open and glance upon whatever horrors it might summon to trouble them for a fourth night. She took the sash from her curtain and bound the book shut with it. After thrusting it into a shoulder bag, she quickly dressed, making sure to put on her riding boots.

She stomped back down the stairs and on her way to the yard, she grabbed her father's rifle at his feet and the pouch of ammunition from the table.

"What are you going to do?" Henry spluttered through his fingers.

"I'm going to see a man about a dog, Father. And then

I'm going to put an end to this."

**

Once the horse was bridled and saddled up, she slung the rifle over her back and road out of the village with as much haste as Richard could muster. When the fallen stones came into sight, she tugged on his reign, leaping out of the saddle before he had even stopped, and led him to a nearby tree. She lashed him to a sturdy branch and patted his nose.

"Stay here, my friend," she said. "I don't want you anywhere near him when he comes."

Slowly, carefully, checking the track in all directions as she crept, she approached the centre of the crossroads. When she reached it, she unhooked the rifle from her back and loaded a shell from her pouch into the firing chamber. She pulled out the book, untied the sash around it and threw it into the centre of the crossing, where it fell open on the first page.

"Andromalius!" she screamed. "Show yourself!"

Nothing, except the echo of her voice and the rattle of startled birds fleeing from the treetops.

"Andromalius! I know you can hear me! Come out and face me like a man." She paused and smirked. "Or are you too afraid of a mere girl?"

Still nothing, except a nervous whinny from Richard.

"Oh, I wish he would..."

"Hello, Ellie."

She spun around. There he was, grinning like the cat who'd cornered the mouse.

"You!" she roared, levelling the rifle at his chest.

"Nobody calls me that except my father."

"Is that how you greet an old friend? How about 'Hey Andy, how's it going? Thanks for the book, dude! I really liked it, especially the twist ending.' You know? That kind of thing." He stepped towards her.

She raised the rifle to his face.

"You're upset, aren't you?" He held up his hands and took a step back, stumbling on loose gravel as he did so. He reached for one of the boulders to steady himself but he fell to his knees.

As he clambered back to his feet, his trouser leg rode partway up his calf and Eleanor's view was drawn to a maroon stain, surrounding an oval of angry-looking puncture marks on his bare leg.

"Bess," she whispered, lowing the gun. Richard snorted behind her and she turned her head to check on him.

In the split second that her attention was elsewhere, Andromalius crossed the circle with unnatural speed and gripped her by the throat.

She choked and gasped for air as she found herself getting lost in raven black eyes; a gaze as boundless and Stygian as a river on a moonless night.

He lifted her up, gripping her tightly beneath her chin until her feet left the floor. She kicked at him but the blows just glanced away.

"Here's what's going to happen. I'm going to put you down, and you're going to be a good, obedient little girl. You're going to pack up your bag, ride good old reliable Richard here all the way home and sit down with a nice cup of tea - you English really do love your tea - and a book - my book. And when I come to you tonight - and I *will* come to you - I'll finally be free, and Ellie... Oh, dear, clever, feisty, misguided Ellie... You and your precious daddy will be the first to face my wrath."

He threw her to the floor and she tumbled sprawling to the grass at the side of the crossroads. She coughed and wheezed, sucking in mouthfuls of air. She cast him a glance so full of hatred and intent to harm that his smile dropped for the briefest moment and he took a step back.

"I'll kill you before you cross the yard," she croaked, rubbing her throat.

"Yeah, good luck with that." He stumbled again, holding a hand out to stop himself from falling forward.

Eleanor looked on aghast as Andromalius seemed to be supporting his weight on nothing but thin air.

"Oh, I see now," she said, grinning. "You're trapped. You can only leave your prison for a short while each night after I open that accursed book, and only in the form of whatever is in the story. Well, I'll never read another word."

Andromalius straightened his tie, ran his fingers through his hair and pulled himself up to his full height, towering over her and blocking out the sun as he grinned that horrible, charismatic, smug, hungry grin.

"You stupid girl. It's too late for that. You set the wheels of my release in motion as soon as you signed your name over to me. You only made me stronger when you breached our contract by closing the book before the end so whether you finish the book or not, my story *will* be completed. The last three nights were just a taster of what's to come. And believe me, you don't want the story to go unfinished, because Bess," he poked out his bottom lip and twisted his fists under his eyes. "Poor, sweet, loyal Bess won't be there to protect you from the next meeting with - I really should come up with a cool-sounding name for when I'm in my half-man-half-fox phase - shall we call him Vulpine? Yes. Let's. Anyway - I digress. Bess won't be there to save Daddy in his sleep a second time. But you?" He looked her up and down. "I think I'll keep you as a pet. For a good long while. Ouch!"

He grimaced and rubbed at his injured calf, cursing under his breath. "Stupid mutt had it coming after what she did to me in my weakened state."

Eleanor shook with rage, gritting her teeth and clenching her fists so tight that her nails drew spots of blood from her palms. She climbed to her feet, picked up the rifle and aimed it again at Andromalius's chest. He stepped towards her but she loosed the shot before he could get any closer.

He stopped, reached into his jacket pocket and pulled out the still-steaming bullet along with the paper she'd signed, which now had a perfectly circular hole through the centre.

"Excellent shot." He peered at her through the hole, poked his finger into it, and then he sighed. "But I did really like this suit. I'm going to make you pay, you troublesome little girl. But first, how about a little spoiler from tonight's story? I think you'll like it."

He turned away from her and walked back to the centre of the crossroads, hand outstretched to pick up the book. "Once upon a time, there was a devilishly handsome *man*, and his name was..."

"Andromalius," she called as she loaded another bullet into the chamber and levelled the gun at him again.

He whipped his head around to her, teeth bared and black eyes brimming with malice. "Stubborn, foolish girl," he crowed. "You've seen that you can't hurt me. Just give up and admit that you're beaten! There can still be a happily ever after - of sorts - if you put your primitive weapon down."

"You talk too much," she said. "So I only have three things to say to you. One: I haven't been a little girl for a very long time. Two: you are not even half a man. And..." She slowly lowered the gun.

Andromalius cackled in triumph, but his laugh was cut short when he realised that Eleanor was only lowering the gun to aim it at something else.

She tightened her grip on the trigger.

His eyes flew wide open, dawning horror slowly replacing the gleeful malevolence. "Wait! What are you doing?"

"I'm finishing the story *my* way."

"No!" He raced towards her, his hand outstretched.

She pulled the trigger as he leapt forward, reaching for the bullet, which whooshed between his open fingers before he could close them. As he sailed through the air, he twisted his head towards the crossroads, to see the slug plough through the pages of the book, sending a plume of tattered paper blasting into the air. He turned back to her, his face contorted with surprise and fear.

"I'll find a way out eventually, and when—"

"Let me finish, you pig!" Eleanor roared.

Andromalius crumbled to ash before he hit the floor.

The riven contract gently drifted back and forth on the breeze amongst the confetti shower of shredded paper until it settled on top of what had once been Eleanor's tormentor. It burst into bright green flames.

"Three: I prefer science journals, you dull-witted buffoon. I never did like fairy tales."

ABOUT THE AUTHOR

Paul Childs's first short story, *The Conductor,* originally appeared in *Hallowscream* (*a* fan made tribute to 1980s horror comic *Scream!*) in 2015.

In 2021, an expanded version of the same story was included in *Horrifying Tales* by Greenteeth Press and his alien invasion tale, *In Memoria Furem, appeared* in their anthology *Tales To Survive The Stars.* In May 2022, Greenteeth published *Tales From Badgers Crossing*, his first full-length collection.

In 2021, he recorded his story *Sunday Shoes* for Peter Laws's Patron only podcast and in 2020 and 2022 he hosted a pair of online charity storytelling nights, to raise money for MS Society and The Trussell Trust.

Paul's work has also appeared in *Strange Abrasions* from Comma Press and *The Accidental Time Travelers Collective Vol. 1*, an anthology published by a group of authors who share a common love for time travel fiction.

He runs and writes for the pop-culture website *World Geekly News* and has also written several nonfiction pieces for sites including *Den Of Geek*, *Ginger Nuts Of Horror*, *Horrified* and *Folklore Thursday*. Between 2018 and 2020 he wrote a regular column on movie songs for *Film Stories* print magazine.

When he's not writing, Paul enjoys horror and action films, listening to 1980s rock music (and playing it on one of his many guitars), tasting single malt whisky, collecting vintage action figures, and messing about with Lego.

ALSO FROM PAUL CHILDS

Tales From Badgers Crossing

You can read further adventures of Debbie, Tim, Bert, Cally, Ernie Hunt, Liz Wilde and even The Conductor in Paul's debut collection, **Tales From Badgers Crossing.** Eleven short stories of "Spooky Nostalgia" all set in or linked to *The Most Haunted Town in Britain.*

With a foreword by Peter Laws, author of the *Matt Hunter* crime novels, *Fortean Times* columnist and the host of *Frightful* podcast.

Praise for Tales From Badgers Crossing:

"Childs has a remarkably easy-to-read writing style, with a very light touch. He's developed an incredibly welcoming narrative voice that invites you in and pulls you through the stories effortlessly."

Andrew Lyall, author of *17 Stories of Death & Desire* and *The Well At The End Of The World*

"The prose crackles with energy and is engaging in the way it delivers such many and varied concepts."

Matt Adcock, author of *Complete Darkness* and *Battlemages Don't Brush Their Teeth*

"Whimsical, charming and a little mysterious, Badger's Crossing is a delightfully earnest conundrum of a town, and visitors should heed the warning – Be Careful How You Go!"

Gemma Amor, Bram Stoker Award nominated author of *Dear Laura*, *Full Immersion* and *The Once Yellow House*

Tales From Badgers Crossing, published by Greenteeth Press, is available to buy now as a paperback or eBook. Visit PaulChilds.co.uk for more details.

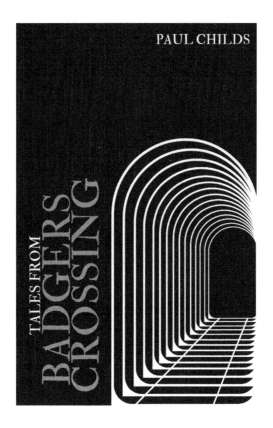

COMING SOON

The Convergence: A Badgers Crossing Novella by Paul Childs

Sergeant Lisa "Cally" Callaghan gets all the weird cases. The ones that nobody else at the station wants - or dares - to investigate.

A horrific incident during an illegal live stream from the disused 1970s transportation hub that was once the jewel in the crown of Badgers Crossing's post-war regeneration programme, Cally and her protégé Constable Zainab Adhikari inadvertently uncover a mystery far more terrifying and ancient than they could ever have imagined.

A horror story from Paul Childs featuring a combination of Police Procedural, Found Footage, Folk Horror and post-war Brutalist architecture.

The Convergence will also feature a brand new bonus story.

Available from Autumn, 2023

The Convergence

A Badgers Crossing novella by

Paul Childs

Excerpt from *The Convergence*

"One day Morty comes along and says 'Who's coming to The Stones', as they used to call them. I declined, as did many of the others, despite the ribbing we received. All apart from Keith.

"They disappeared into the grass. When they didn't come back, even after we called their names out, the rest of us decided to go home.

"The next day we were all around Keith in the playground before school. 'What was it like?', 'What did you do?' but he didn't want to talk about it. We made our way into assembly and I realised something wasn't right when I saw a policeman on the stage with the headmaster.

"After we'd sung a hymn, the copper was introduced to us. He gave us a talking to about playing in safe places and told us all about the dangers of quarries, farmyards and building sites - all the kinds of places we loved. He reminded us that there was a war on and the last thing the emergency services needed if there was an air raid was having to round up a gang of unruly kids.

"He said that one of the boys from the big school, Joseph Morton, hadn't come home the night before, and encouraged us to come to the headmaster's office if we had any information about his whereabouts. He assured us we wouldn't get into trouble. They just wanted to get Morty home to his worried parents.

"Keith was never the same after that day. He wouldn't tell us what he saw, even when I asked over thirty years later in... when was it? Seventy-five?"

"Seventy-six," Zainab said.

"Do you mind if I ask how old you are Constable?" Bert said.

"Not at all. I'm twenty-two. Why?"

"You've only ever known life with that place closed down. You've never been inside it, or stood waiting for a bus there."

Zainab shook her head.

"I have," Cally cut in. "It was always cold. Even in the summer. Buses kept breaking down, passengers suddenly taking ill, bags mysteriously disappearing from luggage holds. Companies refused to include it on their routes after a while. I remember reading a piece on it when I was on my paper round. After the last bus left in 1993 they bricked it all up. The car park lasted three more years but when the lift crashed down to the ground floor, that was the final straw."

"Aye," said Bert. "They never found the couple who were caught on camera going into the elevator. Only a little bit of blood in the wreck of the carriage.

"That place, even before they built it, has haunted me almost my whole life. I'd like to live out what little time I have left safe in the knowledge that it's been sent back into whichever Godforsaken hole it crawled out of."

Printed in Great Britain
by Amazon